FRAMED

F-BOMB: CURVY VIGILANTES, BOOK TWO

MARY E THOMPSON

Framed

F-BOMB: Curvy Vigilantes, book two

Copyright © 2022 Mary E Thompson

Cover Copyright © 2022 Mary E Thompson

Cover Photo from depositphotos, Copyright © nejron

Break (Mask) from depositphotos, Copyright © K3star

Published by BluEyed Press

Ebook ISBN: 978-1-953879-29-5

Print ISBN: 978-1-953879-30-1

Audiobook ISBN: 978-1-953879-31-8

❀ Created with Vellum

F-BOMB: CURVY VIGILANTES

Say hello to the Curvy Vigilantes, a group of plus-size women who protect their city. They have no training, but they don't need it. All they need is the desire to right wrongs and to protect the ones they love... and maybe some help from the men strong (and smart) enough to fall for these kick-ass curvy women.

F-BOMB: CURVY VIGILANTES
Forsaken (subscriber exclusive)
Fury
Framed
Feign
Fierce
Fatal
Flee
Fracture
Fear
Faith

SUBSCRIBE NOW AT MARYETHOMPSON.COM

To Mary... for always encouraging me to believe in myself and helping me to be the best version of me I can possibly be. Thank you.

1

———

Who knew a crushed skull would bleed so much?

Jessica German looked down at her best friend. Karli's dark hair was wet where her head had been smashed in. Blood pooled beneath her, soaking into the carpet and dripping from the ends of her curls. The formerly appealing smell of piping hot pizza Jessica carried into the apartment blended with the metallic scent of blood in the air.

So much blood.

What was she supposed to do? Try to stop the bleeding. Jessica hurried to the kitchen and grabbed a towel, then rushed back and pressed it to Karli's head. The softness of her broken skull sent a sickening flush over Jessica's body. That wasn't normal.

Jessica reached down and pressed her shaking fingers against Karli's neck. That's what you were supposed to do, right? Did she suck at that, or was there no pulse? Jessica reached up to her own neck and felt the rapid thump of her heart beating. She repositioned her fingers on Karli's neck.

Still nothing.

Jessica was supposed to be there to tell Karli all about

her first date with Braden, the man Jessica had been crushing on for years, a date that didn't end until early that morning with a promise for date two very soon, but Karli was dead. Dead dead, not dead tired or dead drunk, but head smashed in, brains visible kind of dead.

Jessica's stomach flipped and threatened to add to the messy scene. Instead, she choked it back and dug out her phone, her gaze never leaving Karli's lifeless body.

"Nine-one-one. What is your emergency?" the far-too-chipped voice on the other end of the line asked.

"My friend is dead. She's...she's not moving." Tears threatened Jessica's cheeks. She wiped them away before they blurred Karli's figure, just in case she moved. Just in case she was only pretending to be dead.

"Okay. What is your address?"

"Nine-thirty-seven Mist Avenue. Apartment Three-B."

"What happened?" the woman snapped.

"I don't know. I was just bringing dinner. Her head... There's so much blood."

"Why did you kill her?"

"What? I didn't kill her!" Jessica shouted. Why would she kill her best friend?

"Then why did it take you so long to call?"

"What are you talking about?"

"There are already officers on their way to the apartment. One of the neighbors said they heard shouting and a woman with short, dark hair ran out, covered in blood. Where are you, Ms. German?"

"How do you know my name?" Every hair on Jessica's body stood on end. An icy chill swept over her. She looked around like she was being watched.

"The name the phone is registered to comes up when you call. Are you at home?"

"No. I'm..." Jessica stared down at Karli. She couldn't admit she was at Karli's. Then the police would arrest her. But they were already on the way.

"Ms. German, stay where you are. The police need answers from you."

Jessica tapped her screen to end the call. She looked at her friend once more, choking back tears. Karli was dead. There was nothing Jessica could do for her friend.

Sirens echoed in the distance. Not close, but Jessica knew they were coming for her. For Karli. To try to save what was already gone. And to take Jessica to jail for something she didn't do.

She couldn't sit there and wait. She did nothing wrong. They would figure it out. But she had to go. Now.

The hallway was empty when Jessica walked into it. Her options were stairs or an elevator, and Jessica chose the stairs. If she was lucky, she could get down them and out of the building before anyone saw her, and before the police arrived.

"Excuse me," a man said, bumping into her as she turned the corner on the first floor. "Are you okay? You're bleeding."

"I'm fine," Jessica said quickly, looking down at where Karli's blood had stained her jeans and tee.

"Are you sure? That's a lot of blood."

Jessica ignored the man and kept going. She raced the rest of the way down the stairs and pushed the emergency exit door for residents only and escaped into the alley next to the building.

She pulled her purse in front of the bloodstain and rushed to her car. She'd just closed the door when two police cars and an ambulance screeched to a stop at the front door.

Jessica didn't waste time pulling away from the curb and turning in the opposite direction. She needed to change and find out what the hell was going on.

BRADEN WRIGHT KEPT his phone next to him, waiting for any piece of news. He hated leaving his bed that morning, especially when it was full of a warm, curvy, beautiful woman, but Jessica said she understood and didn't hesitate to get up and leave when Braden's closest friend, Wray, called and asked Braden to watch the boys.

Braden didn't know everything that was going on with Wray and his wife, but he knew enough to know Stacey could be in deep shit. The one and only text Wray sent said he was heading to the police station because Stacey was arrested.

It was almost laughable to think of Stacey Allen ever hurting anyone, but people did crazy things when someone they cared about was in danger.

"Uncle Braden, can we play a game?" Joey asked.

"Absolutely, bud. What do you want to play?"

"Outside?"

"Let's go." Braden smiled at the boys. He loved them like they were his own. Wray was his family, and Wray's boys were Braden's heart. After his tumultuous childhood, Braden wasn't sure he'd ever have a family, but when Wray and Stacey got married, he was a little jealous. He wanted that, too, but he never admitted it out loud.

He'd also never met anyone he could picture a life with. Until last night.

"I throw to you, and you throw to Evan, and he throws to me," Joey said.

Braden looked at three-year-old Evan and shook his head. "How about you throw to me, and Evan can toss back when he's in the mood?"

Joey shrugged. He was a good big brother. Braden was the youngest of four and knew how important it was to have older siblings that were amazing. He had three of them. He was closest to Taylor, the oldest, but the other two were always there for him if he needed it.

Joey tossed the soft football to Braden, then caught it when Braden threw it back. Evan ran around in the yard, jumping up like he was going to catch the ball when it sailed over his head.

"Do you want to play?" Braden asked.

"Yeah," Evan said. "I likes football."

Braden nodded and gently tossed the ball to Evan. He reached for it and missed by a mile, the ball sliding between his arms and hitting him in the chest before landing on the ground. He picked it up and threw it back to Braden, then went to his swing set and scrambled up the stairs toward the slide.

Braden kept an eye on Evan and played catch with Joey. He stifled a yawn, the product of a long night between the thighs of Jessica German, and grinned.

"Why are you smiling?" Joey asked.

Braden quickly schooled his features, but it was obviously too late. "I was just thinking about something a friend said yesterday."

"What friend?"

"Her name is Jessica."

"What did she say?"

Braden thought quickly to come up with something other than the sexy words Jessica whispered when he sank into her the first time. "I've never come that hard." His dick swelled with his chest when she confessed that. He didn't think she meant to say it, but all it did was make him want to try harder to please her.

"She said she could throw a ball harder than me."

"My mommy can't throw very hard. She said she's not that strong, but she can still carry my brother, so I know she's strong," Joey said.

"Your mommy is very strong. She's smart and creative and beautiful, too."

"Do you like my mommy?" Joey asked.

"Very much. She's a good friend of mine. I'm very happy she married your daddy because he loves her a lot."

"He almost messed it up, but he fixed it again."

Braden smiled. "Yes, he did. Are you guys hungry? Want a snack or lunch or something?"

Both boys cheered and raced for the door. Food was always a good distraction with them. They were always hungry.

It wasn't too long after lunch when Wray and Stacey got home. Stacey went straight upstairs to shower, and Wray took over kid duty. He promised to get in touch later and give Braden an update. Braden understood that meant he couldn't talk in front of the boys. And likely also meant Wray wouldn't be in for their shift at the fire station that night.

Braden made his way out with the promise that he would always be there to help with the boys if Wray or Stacey needed him.

Sleep was important when Braden was working overnight, but sleep evaded him. His pillow smelled like Jessica, and he couldn't stop his mind from replaying their night over and over until his alarm went off.

He dragged himself into the shower, then headed to

work. He sent Jessica a text, but by the time he got to work, there wasn't a reply. He pushed it out of his mind and started his shift.

A call came in early in the shift, then the team settled in for dinner. Braden went to the weight room to get out some of his pent up energy before eating. When he joined the rest of them, they were deep in conversation.

"Hey Wright, why is your date on the news?" asked Marcinko.

"What are you talking about?"

"That woman who works for your sister? Didn't you go out with her?"

"Yeah. So?"

"She killed someone. She's on the news." Powers pointed to the TV screen where the news was on as Braden opened his mouth to argue.

Then snapped it shut.

"Police are looking for a suspect in the murder of a local woman tonight. Karli Sloane's body was found in her apartment this afternoon. She was an art therapist and loved by her patients. A woman named Jessica German was seen fleeing Ms. Sloane's apartment shortly before police arrived. This picture was taken from security cameras in Ms. Sloane's apartment building. If anyone has any information about Ms. German's whereabouts, you are asked to call the police."

Braden had seen some of the worst humanity had to offer in his years since joining the fire department, but finding out the woman he spent the night with was a murderer was more than a little shocking.

Braden's phone buzzed in his pocket. He wasn't sure he wanted to answer it, but when he saw it was his sister, he left the break room to find some privacy from his nosy coworkers. "I saw."

"It's not true, Braden."

"How do you know?"

Jessica had been Taylor's assistant for years. They were close, even more since Taylor's boyfriend knocked down a few of the walls she used to keep people at bay. Braden would forever be grateful to Dex for how happy he made Taylor. If anyone deserved it, it was her.

"She's not that kind of person. You know this. You know her."

"Do I? Do you? Come on, Tay-Tay, do we ever really know anyone? Do we need to talk about Dad?"

"Dad is a monster. He's different. This is Jessica. You were with her last night. How did she seem after your date?"

Braden hardened at the thought. Their date was supposed to be dinner. Braden thought Jessica was sweet and smart, and Taylor wore him down, saying she thought they'd be good together. Braden asked Jessica out to get his sister off his back. He never expected to connect with Jessica the way he did. To not want the night to end and invite her back to his place. Or to carry her to his room and taste every inch of her sexy, curvy body.

"Braden? Are you still there?"

"Yeah. I'm here. Sorry. She was fine. I don't know what you want me to say. Did she look like she was going to leave my place and kill her best friend? No."

"Whoa, wait. I thought you were meeting at the restaurant. Why was she at your house?"

"Um, well..."

"Hey! Give that back!" Taylor shouted, her voice far away.

"You do not have to tell your sister anything," Dex said.

He moved in with Taylor shortly after they got together, and Dex was like another brother to Braden. One who wasn't afraid to run interference between the siblings.

"She's going to be pissed you stole her phone."

"She'll get over it, eventually. Listen, for what it's worth, I can't see Jessica doing what they said she did. She's too sweet of a person. She's not the type to snap, and she's not the type to plan something like this. Trust me."

Braden really wanted to believe Dex and Taylor. Taylor had a knack for seeing who a person truly was, which made her an amazing boss and business owner. Dex was a former SEAL with an undeniable talent for reading people.

But no matter how much Braden wanted to believe them, and how much he thought the same, what he couldn't understand was... "Where is she? If she was there, she had to know the police would want to talk to her. Why wouldn't she stay to answer questions?"

Dex sighed, as if he expected the question. "I can't answer that. Have you spoken to her?"

"Not since she left this morning."

"This... I am not going to repeat that, but do you really think that little of the," his voice dropped to a whisper, "woman you spent the night with?"

"I don't know, man. I'm going to try to call her. See if she'll talk to me. Tell me what's going on."

"I know you like to follow the rules, and I do, too, but you have to understand not everyone feels as though they can. We don't know what was going through her mind, but maybe she's a witness and doesn't think she's safe."

"They said she's a suspect."

"I know, but Braden, don't jump to conclusions yet."

"Too late."

Dex sighed. "Do you want us on this?" Dex was part

owner of a group of former SEALs who helped protect the borders. Among other things.

"This isn't what you guys do."

"We find people, and we protect people, and we uncover the truth. We will find Jessica if you want us to."

Braden shook his head before he answered. "No, it's fine. I'm sure there's an explanation."

"I'm sure there is. If we hear anything, we'll let you know."

"Thanks. And thanks for the wrath you're about to face with Taylor."

Dex chuckled. "I can handle it. Keep in touch."

Braden nodded and hung up. He didn't feel any better.

He called Jessica, but it went to voicemail. He wasn't sure what he was expecting, but it was still a disappointment to hear her recorded voice asking him to leave a message.

"Hey, Jessica. I don't know what's going on, but I hope you're safe. If I can help you, call me."

Braden hung up and sent a text with a similar message, then stared at his phone. Now what?

The voices and sounds of the rest of the crew filtered through the open space to him. Braden's stomach growled. It was going to be a long night. Even longer if he didn't eat.

He ignored the other guys and carried a bowl of chili to the end of the table. A few of them gave him a side-eye, but he focused on his food instead of them. When he was done, he put his bowl and spoon in the dishwasher and went to the bunk room to call Jessica again.

No answer. Again. He didn't bother to leave another message.

Where was she? And why didn't she talk to the police? If she didn't kill Karli, why was she running from Karli's building? With blood on her clothes.

2

———

JESSICA WATCHED THE HOUSE AS THE LIGHTS WENT OFF ONE BY one. She shivered in the chilly evening air. It was only going to get worse as the night wore on. But Jessica didn't care about herself at that moment. She had a more important mission.

Finally, the light in the upstairs bedroom went on. Full light, then softer, like a lamp. Jessica hated what she had to do, but she knew it was necessary.

She crept from her hiding place behind the playhouse in the backyard. The high fence meant she was hidden from the neighbors. She was safe. As safe as she could be when she was on the run.

She tiptoed up to the deck and peeked inside. Stacey was the only one there, which meant Wray was upstairs with the boys. Exactly how Jessica hoped the night would go.

She knocked on the backdoor and waited, knowing what she was doing would scare Stacey. But Jessica had no choice. When there was no light and no sound, Jessica knocked again, this time identifying herself.

"Stacey? It's Jessica."

The door flew open. Stacey was backlit by the inside lights. She reached to the side and set something down. A knife.

Jessica's heart sank. She didn't mean to scare her friend. She only wanted to help Raina.

"Jessica? What are you...? Is that blood?"

Jessica hadn't thought about the way she looked. When she ran from Karli's apartment, she intended to go home and change, but before she got there, she changed her mind. The nine-one-one operator knew her name, which meant the police knew where she lived. It wasn't safe to go there.

Instead of going home, Jessica went to an ATM and took out as much cash as she could. Then she ditched her phone and car and spent the rest of the evening on foot, trying to make her way to Stacey's house.

Jessica swiped her hands over Karli's blood, but it didn't do anything. The stains were already set. Just like her friend's fate. "Yeah. Sorry. I just—"

"Come in. Are you hurt? What the hell happened?"

Jessica shook her head. A twig snapped in the night, and she looked toward the noise. It was a risk going to Stacey's. A risk Jessica wouldn't have taken unless she had no other choice. "Do you have a way to get in touch with Raina?"

"Raina? Um, yeah, I have a number for her. Why? What's going on?"

"Karli's dead." Saying the words was the hardest thing Jessica had ever done. She still couldn't believe it was true, but she'd been there. She'd seen it with her own eyes. But she couldn't let the despair get in. If she did, she'd never survive.

"What? How? What?"

"I didn't do it, Stacey. I promise you. It wasn't me."

"Of course not. Why would I ever think that?"

Jessica exhaled, relief exploding from her. She half expected Stacey to think she was guilty. Hell, she half expected Stacey to already know what was going on.

"Karli sent me a text to come over earlier today. She wanted..." She stopped and drew a shaky breath. It should have been a fun night, not a deadly one. "I had a date with Braden last night, and Karli wanted to hear how it went. I was going over there earlier for dinner and movie night, but when I got there..."

Jessica bent at the waist, fighting the pain inside her. Everything hurt. Her best friend was gone, and nothing would ever change that.

"Jessica, come inside. Let's get you cleaned up and into fresh clothes." Stacey reached for her arm, but Jessica twisted out of the way.

"No," she blurted, taking another step back. "I can't. I just... Someone saw me there, I guess. I don't know. I called nine-one-one, but I kind of freaked out because the operator asked me why I killed someone, and I just left, but I was covered in blood, and someone must have seen me leaving Karli's apartment, and now the police have my name and face all over the news because they think I killed my friend, but I didn't, Stacey. I didn't kill her. She was dead when I got there. Her head..." Jessica reached back and touched the back of her skull. "Her head was smashed in, and blood was just everywhere, and oh, my God, Karli's dead. Stacey, she's dead."

"Jessica, please come in. We'll figure this out. I'll call Marcus, and—"

"No," Jessica said. Fear slithered up her spine. She couldn't talk to the police. She couldn't talk to anyone. And she couldn't risk anyone else getting in trouble for helping her. "I can't. I can't put your family in danger. I wouldn't have come here at all, except I was worried about Raina. I don't know where she'll go, or if she's okay. I don't know who killed Karli. It could have been Raina's husband trying to get to her. Or it could have been random. But Karli was so sweet, and I don't know why anyone would want to hurt her."

"We'll figure this out. Where are you staying?" Stacey again reached for Jessica's arm.

Jessica shook her head. "I don't know. And if I did, I wouldn't be able to tell you."

"Why not? I want to help you. Let me help you. Wray and Braden can help. Marcus. We'll—"

"I don't want to involve any of you. Braden... It's not fair to any of you. Just find Raina. Please. Make sure she's safe." Jessica couldn't think about the rest of them. Just Raina. Raina was the reason she took the chance to go to Stacey's. The others...they would be better off without Jessica around. She knew that.

"I will. But Jessica, you don't have to do this alone. We can help you. You can stay at the shelter."

"Marcus lives there. He wouldn't be able to not turn me in."

"Well..." Stacey knew it was true. Her gaze drifted, like she was trying to come up with something.

"I know you want to help, and I appreciate it, but I just came here so you'd know to look for Raina. Okay?" Jessica met Stacey's gaze, hoping Stacey would do what she said. Hoping Stacey could keep Raina safe.

"Okay. Jessica—"

"Hey, Stace," Wray said from inside. "Have you seen my phone?"

Stacey turned to answer him, and Jessica knew it was

time to go. She took off toward the playhouse, ducking behind it while Stacey focused on her husband. "Um, no, but I'll help you look in a minute."

Jessica watched from the darkness as Stacey turned back. She stepped outside, looking around the backyard. Jessica didn't move, she didn't even breathe. Anything could draw Stacey's attention, which would catch Wray's attention.

"Hey. What are you doing outside?" Wray asked, joining Stacey on the porch. Jessica could just barely hear their conversation in the quiet night.

"Um, Jessica was just here."

"Braden's Jessica?" That one kicked Jessica in the chest. She'd wanted to be Braden's Jessica for years, and when she finally had a chance, it was stolen from her.

Stacey nodded, still scanning the yard. "Yeah. And she's in trouble."

Wray followed Stacey's gaze, then grabbed her arm. "Let's go inside and you can tell me what's going on."

Stacey looked around once more, then let Wray pull her inside. The door clicked shut, and the lock snapped into place. Only then did Jessica breathe.

She still didn't move, but she knew they wouldn't be back outside.

A few minutes later, the rest of the downstairs lights went out. The faint glow of a light upstairs shined through one window, then blinked out a minute later. The house was dark. And it was time to move.

BRADEN TRIED to lose himself in a movie on his phone, but he couldn't focus. He thought about going out to look for Jessica, but he had no idea where she would be. The police had her name, which meant they also had her address, details about her car, her job, and had likely already gone through her social media. Where would she go?

Braden shook his head. It didn't matter. He wasn't going to go looking for her. He was working. And leaving in the middle of a shift would put his fellow firefighters at risk.

His phone rang, and he dropped it. He scrambled to pick it up before the call went to voicemail and answered without looking at the screen. "Hello? Jessica?"

"She was just here," Wray said.

"What? Why was she at your house?"

"She came to talk to Stacey."

"Why?"

"She said she didn't kill Karli. Stacey believes her."

"That seems to be the common thread," Braden grumbled.

"You think she did it?"

"I don't know what to think. If she's innocent, where the hell is she?"

"Stacey said she was scared. And covered in blood. She risked coming to our house because she is worried about Raina."

"Who the hell is Raina?"

"Karli had a roommate. Someone who was at the shelter until recently. They were old friends, and when Raina left the shelter, Karli agreed to take her in. Safety in numbers. Anyway, Jessica came here to tell Stacey to get in touch with Raina."

"That doesn't sound like something a guilty woman would do." Braden was on his feet and heading to the office.

"That's what I said, too. I agree she should have gone to the police, but she's probably in shock."

"All the more reason she shouldn't be out there wandering around."

Braden had to find her. He held the phone away from his face and walked into the battalion chief's office. "Sir, I need to run an errand. I'll be back as soon as possible, if that's okay."

The chief nodded. "Keep your phone on you."

"Yes, sir," Braden said, hurrying away from the office and racing toward his truck.

"What are you doing?" Wray barked through the phone.

Braden hoped Wray hadn't overheard, but no such luck. "I'm going to find her. Make her go to the police station."

"Are you sure that's a good idea? You're working."

"Do you really think it's a good idea to let a woman wander the streets alone? Why the hell did you let her leave your house?" Braden spat.

"I didn't know she was here until after she was gone. She knocked on the backdoor when I was putting the boys to bed. Stacey was the only one in the kitchen."

"How did she time that just right?"

"She was probably watching us," Wray said.

"What were you saying about her being innocent?"

"Just because she was watching us doesn't mean she's a killer. She wanted to protect Raina."

"Or she wants to draw her out."

"Why are you going out looking for her if you think she's guilty?"

Braden sighed and turned onto Wray's street. He went slowly, scanning both sides of the road for anyone walking around or hiding behind cars or trees or in backyards. He told himself he was too focused on his task to answer the question Wray asked.

"You know she didn't do this," Wray answered for Braden.

"I don't know anything. But if people don't follow the rules and trust the system, what good is the system?"

"I think you're asking for too much. People are fallible. We do it all the time. That doesn't mean we shouldn't try to be better, but it means we have to accept that we're all different and we all screw up."

"Are you talking about yourself or Jessica?"

"I'm talking about everyone. You're not perfect either."

Braden grunted. He knew he wasn't. Far from it. But he wasn't a killer.

"Jessica isn't a killer," Wray said as though he read Braden's mind. "And until you talk to her, you can't make judgements on what she did. Find her and get answers first."

"And what if I don't like the answers I get?"

"Only you know what you're able to handle, Braden. But don't go to worst case off the bat."

Braden huffed. He didn't like it, but Wray was right. First, he needed to find Jessica.

JESSICA'S EYES FELL SHUT. Blood. Brains. Karli.

She jerked awake, her entire being on high alert. There was a sound. Something. What was it?

She looked around. She couldn't see anyone, but someone was there. Was it the person who killed Karli?

Jessica shivered and wrapped her jacket tighter around her body. It was cold. The cash she got out of the ATM wasn't going to go far, so she was trying to be smart. She bought a cheap string bag so she could carry the tiny amount of things she had with her. She'd ditched her purse, but she kept her wallet and a few personal items. She would give it all up for a warmer coat, but food was more important.

Jessica stood, trying to see in the dark of night. She thought the park would be a good place to spend the night, but she was clearly not the only one. It was busy when she arrived after her visit to Stacey's house. Jessica thought that was good at first, but she quickly realized she was not warmly welcomed.

"Who are you?" a woman asked when Jessica settled onto a bench.

"I'm just looking for a place to rest."

"That's my bench. I've been sleeping there for two years. You don't get to walk in here and claim something as yours."

"Sorry," Jessica said, getting up and moving away. "I didn't realize."

"Yeah, well, someone dressed like you isn't supposed to be here. This ain't no place for you."

"Excuse me?"

"You heard me. This is where we live. We all know each other, and we all watch out for each other. And someone like you comes, all you bring is trouble. We don't want that here."

"I'm not here to cause trouble."

"I didn't say that. I said you bring trouble. You're running from someone, and they gonna find you. And when they do, we're gonna pay for it."

"I'm not trying to cause problems for anyone."

"Yeah? Then get moving. We don't want you here."

"Where am I supposed to go?"

The woman shrugged. "You think I care?"

Jessica took a few steps away and turned away from the

woman. She grumbled to someone else about people like Jessica ruining what they had.

Hot tears stung her eyes and ran down her cheeks. Jessica had never felt so alone in her life. She wandered around the park for an hour, letting the people who lived there settle for the night. When they did, she found a tree that didn't have someone resting against it and sat down.

She didn't mean to fall asleep.

If sleep brought memories of Karli, Jessica would rather avoid that, anyway. She paced around the park again, ignoring the people who glared at her. It had to be getting close to daybreak, which meant the city would wake up soon.

Jessica left the park and walked. She was grateful she'd been wearing sneakers when she ditched her life and went on the run. They were comfortable and could hold up to walking for hours and hours.

Jessica walked, pretending she was exploring the city. She kept her head down and her hood up and wrapped her coat tight around her body. If she didn't think about how cold she was or how little money she had in her pockets, she could almost pretend she was just sightseeing for the day.

With the morning came some warmth. Jessica debated getting a coffee and eventually decided it was a necessary splurge. Normally, she wouldn't think twice about grabbing a cup of coffee to go, but when she was living on cash and sleeping on the streets, everything was different.

Her usual places had cameras and chatty employees. It made Jessica feel soft and gooey inside when she walked in and they knew her order, or at least recognized her face. When she was supposed to be hiding and risked going to jail, she couldn't go anywhere someone might recognize her.

There was a convenience store a few blocks away. Jessica

debated, again, if it was worth the price for a cup of coffee, but she decided it was. Especially if the place had a bathroom.

She asked if she could use the restroom as soon as she walked in. The clerk said it was for customers only, and Jessica said she didn't want to bring her coffee into the bathroom. The clerk turned her nose up, but pointed toward the back.

The bathroom was dingy, dark, and disgusting, but it had soap and a toilet. Jessica tried to remember she was just as disgusting as the bathroom and that she had no right to turn her nose up at the place. When she finished in the bathroom, she thanked the clerk and got a cup of coffee. She added a bagel and the biggest bottle of water they had, then paid and left the store.

The coffee was barely worth the dollar it cost, but it was warm and full of caffeine, so she tolerated it. Jessica drank while she walked, picking off pieces of her bagel every so often and trying to fill the empty space inside her where Karli used to exist.

It was useless, but she tried.

Through the day, Jessica walked. While she walked, she replayed the day and tried to piece together what happened.

She told Stacey someone must have seen her leave, but that wasn't the real problem. Someone saw her arrive. The nine-one-one operator knew Karli was dead. She knew Jessica was there. She knew too much. For a second, Jessica wondered if she could have been involved, but that was highly unlikely.

But someone knew something.

Whoever called nine-one-one had to have seen Jessica. They had to have known she was in the building. In the five minutes or so it took to climb the stairs to Karli's apartment, someone saw Jessica and called nine-one-one. Someone saw her and lied to nine-one-one. Because the only way they knew she would have blood on her clothes was if they were in Karli's apartment.

She shivered at the thought. Could someone else have been in there? Could the killer have been in there when Jessica was?

Her stomach flipped. She stopped and took a deep breath, then shook her head.

No. If the killer was in the apartment when Jessica was, she would have heard them call nine-one-one. The apartment wasn't that big. She definitely would have heard someone.

Which brought Jessica back to someone saw her walking in. Most likely the person who killed Karli. Anyone else wouldn't have known to point the finger at Jessica. It had to have been the killer.

But who could it have been?

Jessica rolled the question around in her mind for the rest of the day. She ignored the gnawing hunger in her belly and avoided busy places in the city. When evening rolled around again, she found an alley between two businesses that were closed for the night. She didn't like the idea of getting trapped in there if someone else came in, but she wasn't going to stay long. Just a few minutes to rest.

3

———

DAY THREE, AND JESSICA WAS NO CLOSER TO FIGURING anything out. She was getting discouraged. And hungry and tired and heartbroken. She wanted her bed and a shower and her friends. She wanted someone to talk to. She wanted Karli alive again.

Jessica was sure the police would have seen the videos already. There was a camera in the lobby of Karli's apartment building that would show the time Jessica entered the building. And they should have the call log from nine-one-one. They should know when she called, and when the other person called.

The only thing they didn't have was when she left the building. Because she went out the side door. But Jessica knew that was small compared to the other things. If it took her five minutes to walk up the stairs, there was no way she was in the building long enough to have killed Karli by the time the other person called it in.

Unless she took the elevator.

Jessica wanted to scream. She couldn't even convince herself she was innocent, and she knew she was! Going to the police would have sealed her fate. So, she had to find proof.

Especially since she was still a wanted woman.

Her face was on the front-page of every local newspaper. When she went into any convenience store, she was greeted by the security camera footage of her entering Karli's building. One paper showed the footage of Jessica getting cash from the ATM in her blood-covered clothes.

She didn't paint a picture of innocence.

The one thing Jessica wanted to know more than anything else was if Raina was safe. She couldn't risk seeking out Stacey again, so all Jessica could do was hope Stacey had gotten to Raina before her ex did. Jessica had no proof Raina's ex killed Karli, but she had no reason to believe he didn't either.

All Jessica knew was someone killed her friend, and that someone was trying to convince everyone else that Jessica was the guilty one. And unfortunately for her, they were succeeding.

FOUR DAYS. It had been four days with zero information about Jessica. Braden was starting to lose his mind.

"What the hell is wrong with you?" Wray snapped at him. "You've got to get your head in the game."

Braden glared at his best friend. Wray was right, but he hated it. He hated every second of Jessica being gone.

The worst was the gnawing part of him that wouldn't let go of the fear that she was guilty. Everyone around him was trying to convince him she was innocent, but he couldn't fit that piece of information together with an explanation for why she ran, and why she was still on the run.

You don't run if you're innocent.

The fire truck pulled up to a scene, and Braden shoved all thoughts of Jessica out of his head. The owners of the house didn't care what was going on in his life. They cared if he was present enough to do his job. And he had no choice but to be.

Wray stuck close to Braden, pulling him back when Braden was going to step forward and volunteer to go into the house. "We're staying outside. I can't risk you losing focus in there."

Braden grumbled. He was a professional, but one little thing could get both of them killed. If Wray didn't trust him, Braden needed to listen to his partner.

Wray grabbed the end of the hose, leaving Braden to support the middle. His muscles ached after almost an hour of shooting water at the structure that was more shell than house. Smoke poured into the early morning air, making the sky look dark and cloudy instead of bright and sunny like it had been when they left the station.

Another hour and they were dirty, sweaty, and tired and heading back to the station. The fire was out, and the family was safe, but their home was gone. Destroyed by a candle stacked on top of a newspaper.

Braden removed his turnouts and made sure he had gear ready for the next call. His mind raced with the excitement of the call over, and instead of heading to the showers with the rest of the crew, he went to the weight room.

The TV on the wall broadcast news around the clock. Normally, Braden could ignore it, but as soon as he picked up his first set of hand-weights, Jessica's face flashed on the screen.

"Local woman Jessica German is still missing. Police are asking for help from anyone who may have seen Ms.

German in the last four days. She's five-five with green eyes. She was last seen wearing jeans and a gray tee. Ms. German is suspected of killing a former friend and classmate, Karli Sloane. We spoke to an old friend of both women for more on this developing story."

The picture changed. Braden leaned back to watch. The picture of Jessica was the same one the news had been sharing for days, but a story? That was new.

A woman was on the screen, staring at the camera like she was walking the runway instead of on a video call.

"Jessica and Karli were more like enemies than friends. Karli was sweet and confident and knew what she wanted to do with her life. Jessica was jealous of that. She told me once that she hated Karli. I'm not surprised it came to this. The only thing I wish is I could go back and tell someone about Jessica's anger. Maybe Karli would be alive if I'd been brave enough to stand up to Jessica all those years ago."

Braden snorted. That woman clearly didn't know Jessica at all. She didn't have an anger problem. She'd never hurt Karli.

Braden stopped what he was doing, his mind no longer listening to the woman droning on and on about how horrible Jessica was. He set the weights down. Shit. He'd convinced himself Jessica might have done something, but he knew that wasn't possible.

He dug into his pocket and pulled out his phone. The messages he'd sent Jessica had gone unanswered, unread. He was happy she never saw some of them. He questioned her, once, about what happened. If she'd seen that...

Braden couldn't think about that. He needed help. Help he never wanted to ask for again. Help he still was in debt for. But he had no choice. Looking for Jessica on his own had turned up nothing. He needed someone with more resources.

"Hamilton," Dex said when he answered the phone.

"It's Braden. I need a favor."

"Hang on," Dex said. The phone went silent, then Dex came back on the line. "Sorry. Was in a meeting. What's going on? Is everything okay?"

"No. I need to find Jessica."

"Why? Did something happen?"

"Aside from her being missing, no. I just need to find her. I need to know she's okay."

"She's okay, Braden."

"You don't know that. She could be dead. Maybe that's why the police haven't found her. The person who killed Karli might have killed her, too."

"She's not dead. Do you really think your sister wouldn't ask me to find her?"

"You know where she is?"

Dex sighed. "Not at the moment, but generally, yes. We've been keeping tabs on her."

"Why the fuck didn't you tell me?" Every muscle in his body tightened. He wanted to reach through the phone and pummel Dex.

"I wasn't sure what you would do with the information."

"What the hell does that mean?"

Dex sighed. "My team doesn't believe Jessica had anything to do with her friend's death. Between Taylor and I, they trust us and they trust our opinions. My team has been watching her to make sure she's safe. But sharing that information with someone who isn't sure she's innocent could mean her ending up in police custody."

"You thought I would turn her in," Braden admitted. All his anger blinked away. He was an ass. A heartless one who could have kept Jessica safe but instead didn't believe what he knew about her.

Dex didn't reply, just stayed silent on the other end of the line.

"I know she didn't do this. She couldn't have. She's not like that."

"About fucking time you realized it."

"Dammit, Dex, I just... Why did she run? I know she wouldn't kill Karli, but why did she run?"

"Someone said they saw her entering the building. They called it in before she got to her friend's apartment and gave her description."

"How the hell is that possible?"

"She's being set up."

"By who?"

"We don't know that part yet. Unfortunately, there are no other suspects. We're still trying to get access to the security footage of the building. It should be enough, but if the police are still after Jessica, something isn't right."

"Have you talked to Marcus? Did you tell him this?"

"Captain Patrick can only do so much. His word isn't going to set someone free. Especially when there's no proof she's innocent. And she's in hiding."

"So, he thinks she's guilty?"

"He doesn't know what to think, but he knows if we can't find the person who actually killed Ms. Sloane, Jessica will never be free."

"What happens now?"

"We figure out what actually happened?"

"And Jessica? Do you have a way to communicate with her?"

"No. She doesn't know we've been following her."

"You're following her? Not just watching her?"

"We have someone on her at night so we can pull her out of any situation if it's bad enough. So far it hasn't been. But we have a legal obligation to turn her in if we bring her in, so—"

"So you're leaving her where she is so you can say you don't know anything?"

"Exactly."

"Will you tell me where she is? I'm working until tomorrow, but I want to find her."

"I'll see what I can find out."

"Thanks. And Dex?"

"Yeah?"

"Thank you for watching out for her."

"Thank your sister. She's the one who made it happen."

"I will."

JESSICA WAS cold and scared and angry. The worst of it all was that she was alone. She was used to being on her own, but being alone was different. It was hard to have zero contact with anyone.

The only thing she could do was piece together as much as she could about Karli and that day. Just thinking about it brought bile to her throat. She could still see the back of her friend's head, her dark spiral curls matted down with blood. The feeling of her skull soft under the towel Jessica fruitlessly used to stop the bleeding.

Whoever killed Karli had to have seen Jessica come into the building. What she couldn't figure out was who would want Karli dead? And why?

Jessica walked and thought about everything she did that day. She pushed away thoughts of waking up with

Braden curled around her, his naked body pressed to her back. She couldn't think about that. Not when she wasn't sure she'd ever see him again. No, she had to focus on what happened when she got to Karli's.

A man opened the door for Jessica when she got to the building. He was leaving and held it for her since she was carrying pizza. She tried to recall everything she could about him, but she barely noticed him. There was an older woman with a cane in the lobby when Jessica walked in. She was getting her mail and smiled at Jessica.

She didn't see anyone else until after she found Karli. She had a hard time believing the woman with the cane could have had time to kill Karli and get downstairs that quickly, but what about the man who held the door for her?

Jessica was so lost in her thoughts she wasn't paying attention to where she was going. She'd spent hours walking the streets over the last six days, and she realized she'd been to the area before. On her first night.

What she wasn't sure of was if that was good or bad? Would someone be more likely to recognize her if she'd been there before?

Jessica looked over her shoulder and walked faster. She couldn't shake the feeling she was being followed. It wouldn't surprise her to know she was, but she hoped she could avoid whoever set her up for a little longer. After all, shouldn't they want her alive? If she was dead, they couldn't point the finger at her anymore.

She passed an alley and debated going down it. The last time she snuck down an alley, no one saw her. She couldn't chance it if someone was following her. There was a convenience store a few blocks up. If she could make it there, it would be warm. And there were no cameras in the store. She could wander as long as she wanted.

A man bumped into her, sending her spinning. She rubbed her shoulder as he apologized and hurried off in the direction she came from. It was still busy, but it wouldn't be long before the city started to slumber.

Before Jessica had to move.

Sleeping on the streets was impossible. Every little noise woke her up. She never even slept with a window open before, and the traffic, nature, and other people on the street scared the hell out of her.

It had been five nights since she'd gotten more than a handful of minutes of sleep at a time. Since she felt safe. Since she saw the back of her best friend's head in pieces.

Jessica pushed away the tears and kept moving. Getting caught would mean Karli's killer went free. Jessica was not going to let that happen. She had to keep moving and stay alive.

The light in front of the convenience store shined bright on the dim sidewalk. Jessica shivered in her coat, wondering how she would survive the night. It was supposed to rain. She wasn't prepared for rain. She wasn't prepared for anything.

It still felt like someone was following her, but Jessica went into the convenience store, anyway. Inside, she wasn't alone. Someone would notice if she was dragged away. She would not go quietly.

The warmth hit her squarely in the face. Fall was coming quickly. Normally, Jessica loved fall. The changing leaves, the crisp air, the pumpkin flavored everything. Her stomach growled, reminding her she hadn't eaten much. Her clothes were already big on her. Six days without real food was taking a toll. Sure, Jessica always wanted to lose weight, but not like that.

Her cash was running low, so she had to be careful.

Jessica couldn't use cards or get out more cash. She just had to figure it all out.

She walked toward the back, away from the cashier who wasn't paying any attention anyway. None of the food was appealing, but she was starving and needed something to give her calories. And caffeine. Staying up all night was exhausting.

The chime above the door rang. Jessica tucked herself into a corner, pretending to be debating over her options. She learned quickly to stay away from the beer section if she wanted to hide. She also learned no one ever went down the aisle with motor oil and washer fluid. That was her favorite aisle.

The cashier said something to the customer. Jessica heard the blood rushing through her ears. She prayed no one discovered her. She could pay and go and try to survive another night.

The door opened once more. Jessica glanced up and saw the customer leaving. She breathed a sigh of relief. Whoever it was didn't see her. Her paranoia was getting worse.

Jessica carried her meager items to the register and handed over a few bills. The cashier turned her nose up at Jessica. Yeah, six days without a shower was worse than six days without a real meal.

Jessica grabbed her items and stuffed them in her bag. She pushed through the door and turned toward the park she found that afternoon. If she was lucky, she'd find a tree with thick branches to protect her from some of the rain.

She'd gone a few blocks when she heard footsteps behind her. Fast ones. Running. Right toward her.

Panic climbed in her throat. Fear swamped her. The one thing she didn't have was a weapon, something she really needed to remedy. Braden told her she should carry something. Taylor said the same thing. But Jessica thought being attacked once bought her some karma or something and she didn't have to worry.

No such luck.

Jessica knew she wouldn't be able to outrun whoever was coming toward her. The only thing she could do was fight. Fight back and fight hard.

She turned toward the footsteps, grabbing her bag by the straps. She might not have a weapon, but her bag would hurt at least a little.

"Jessica!" a man's voice said.

She was about to swing, but something told her not to. Something... "Braden?"

"Oh, thank God I found you! I've been looking everywhere for you. Come on." Braden stepped into the light, looking like every last fantasy Jessica had for the last six days and five nights.

She never thought she'd see him again. But it was bittersweet to have him there. If he found her, other people could, too. "I can't. You have to go."

"I'm not leaving you on the street. Stacey told me—"

"She sent you?"

"She told me you're innocent. And that you're alone. Why didn't you come to me?"

"Would you have believed me?" Jessica asked. She needed the answer, but she wasn't sure she was going to like it. Braden was a good man, the best. He was honest and kind and understanding. But he was also the kind of guy who trusted the system and lived by the book.

And the look on his face told Jessica his answer before he opened his mouth. "I don't know."

Jessica shook off his hand and turned. "I'm good on my own."

"Jessica, please."

She turned back to him. "Braden, I get it. I ran. I shouldn't have, but I did. I never thought I'd be accused. I found her. I found my best friend." Tears spilled over her lashes and ran down her cheeks. A sob broke free.

Braden pulled her into his arms, not giving her a chance to fight him. He held her close. He smelled so good. Like grilled cheese and soap. And the man Jessica wanted for years but never thought she could have.

She still couldn't have him.

She pulled back, breaking free of his hold, and wiped her cheeks. "I need to go."

"Jessica, come home with me."

"I don't want to put you in a bad position. I'm a fugitive. You'd be harboring a criminal."

"We both know you're not a criminal."

"Do we? Because you said you weren't sure."

"Dammit, Jessica, I'm sorry. This whole situation is messed up. But I'm not letting you sleep on the street for one more night. I've been looking for you all day. Now, get your ass in my truck and come home with me. Because I can't go another night without knowing you're safe. I need to know you're safe, Jessica."

Jessica looked up at him. She saw the truth of his words in his eyes. He was scared. Maybe as scared as she was. Not just of her being alone, but of what could happen to her.

"Okay," she whispered.

Braden exhaled, his body nearly collapsing. He dragged her against him again and held her tight. His heart beat wildly beneath her ear. His muscles were locked around her. His lips found hers in a gentle kiss. "Thank you."

Jessica nodded and let him lead her back to his truck. Safe. For now.

4

Being able to take a shower felt like the greatest blessing ever. Jessica washed her hair three times and her body four. She never thought she'd be so happy to shave in her life. Then she stood under the hot water until it started to run cold.

She almost felt like herself again when she dried off and got dressed in the clean clothes Braden left for her on the counter. Not once did he say anything about how dirty and gross she was. He just walked her to his room, pulled out a pair of sweats and a tee, apologized for not having underwear for her, then directed her to the bathroom across the hall and closed the door so she could have privacy.

A soft knock on the door made her jump. "Do you need anything?" Braden asked, not opening the door.

"I'm good," Jessica replied, walking to the door and opening it as she spoke.

Braden straightened and took a step back. His gaze slid down her body, then jumped back to her face. He cleared his throat. "Um, are you hungry? I made some dinner while you were in the shower."

Jessica's stomach rumbled in answer. She clapped her hand over it as her cheeks flamed. "I could stand to skip a few meals, but I am hungry."

"You don't need to skip anything. You're perfect," Braden declared.

She smiled shyly at him. She wasn't sure how to behave around him. The last time she saw him, they'd spent the night worshipping each other's bodies. Now she was a fugitive, and he wasn't sure he believed she was innocent.

"Come on. Let's eat. I'm starving." Braden took the decision from her when he reached for her hand. He waited for her to reach out before clasping his fingers around hers and pulling her toward the front of the house.

Braden's house was small and cozy. Jessica loved it when she was there almost a week ago, but being there again, it felt like a sanctuary. He led her past the living room and to the kitchen at the back of the house. She noticed the curtains were closed in the front and most of the lights were off. The kitchen was only lit by a small light above the table where two plates of food waited for them.

"Do you want wine or something to drink?"

"Just water," Jessica said. She needed to stay as healthy as possible. And clear-headed.

Braden carried two glasses of water to the table and set one in front of her. He sat and waited for her to lift her fork before he started eating.

The baked chicken and sautéed vegetables were simple but delicious. After eating mostly snacks from convenience stores, Jessica had almost forgotten how delicious home-cooked food could be.

"This is really good. Thank you."

Braden nodded his thanks and glanced down at her

plate. She was almost finished, and he still had half his food left. "There's more if you're still hungry."

Jessica shook her head. "I shouldn't. I don't think my stomach can take it."

"Tomorrow then."

Jessica nodded even though she knew there wouldn't be a tomorrow. She'd eat, she'd get some sleep, and before dawn, she'd leave. She couldn't risk someone finding her there, and she wouldn't put Braden's career and future in jeopardy.

They finished their food in silence. Jessica glanced up at Braden a few times and found him watching her. He quickly looked away, but she felt like an animal in the zoo. "Why are you staring at me?"

"I wasn't sure I'd ever see you again. I thought you might be dead."

"Thankfully, I seem to be more valuable alive than dead."

"What makes you say that?"

She shrugged. "If I'm dead, and it's obvious that it's foul play, it's harder to make it look like I murdered my best friend."

Braden stilled, staring at her for a long moment.

Jessica refused to let the reality sink in. She knew what she said, but she was still telling herself it wasn't real. That Karli wasn't actually dead. If she let it in, she'd fall apart, and then she'd get caught.

"Why did you run?"

"I don't know." Jessica stared at her empty plate and tried to see anything other than the back of Karli's head soaked in blood. "When I walked in... She was just lying on the ground. And there was so much blood. I'm not even sure how long I stood there staring at her. If I'd reacted faster, maybe she would have survived, but—"

"That's not true. It's likely she was dead before you got there."

"Maybe. But I just... The nine-one-one operator said someone already called it in and the police were on their way. She asked me why I killed Karli, and I just freaked out."

"She asked you that?"

Jessica nodded. "She knew my name, and she knew what I looked like. She said someone called it in and described me. She wanted to know where I was so the police could talk to me. I was standing there, staring at my best friend's brain and being accused of killing her. I panicked. It felt like it was already decided that I was guilty. That whole flight, fright, or freeze thing just made me run. Haven't you ever had that happen?"

Braden shook his head slowly. "I haven't, but with my job I'm always facing scary situations. I think firefighters are wired differently."

"I guess that makes sense."

Braden reached across the table and took her hand. She tried to hold back the tears, but one raced down her cheek. He reached up with his other hand and wiped it away.

"Let's go into the living room. Or are you ready for bed?"

Jessica shook her head. Sleep was pulling at her, but her body was still wound up. After running for so long, she wasn't sure she would be able to sleep, no matter how inviting the idea of a bed was.

Braden led her to the couch and sat down, pulling Jessica down next to him. He wrapped an arm around her shoulders and eased her against his side. "I need you close. I'm sorry if I'm annoying you, but I want you against me if it's okay with you."

Jessica nodded and relaxed. He turned on the TV and found a movie. A comedy. She knew it was for her. Braden was a drama and suspense kind of guy, but she was living drama and suspense and needed to not think about the storm surrounding her.

As the movie played, Jessica struggled to stay awake. She was warm and safe for the first time in almost a week, and her body relaxed into Braden, trusting him to make sure nothing happened to her.

JESSICA'S BODY and breathing grew heavier and heavier. Braden didn't move, letting her fall asleep against his side. When she burrowed in and sighed, he finally let out the breath he'd been holding.

She was safe. She was under his roof, and she was safe.

He knew it wouldn't last. That she wouldn't be able to stay with him for long. He'd been getting regular visits from the police to find out if he'd heard from Jessica. It wouldn't be long before they were back to talk to him again.

But for one night, he could keep her safe.

He waited until the movie ended, then turned off the TV. He eased out from underneath her and checked that all the doors were locked, the kitchen was cleaned up, and the lights were off, then he went back to her.

She'd fallen over on the couch and was sound asleep. She looked peaceful, like she did the weekend before when they'd worn each other out. When life almost made sense. When her best friend wasn't dead.

Braden knew he should be a gentleman and put her in the guest room, but he wanted her in his bed. He wanted to feel her move all night and know she was there with him.

He didn't know how long it would be before he saw her again, and he didn't want to miss a thing.

He leaned over in front of the couch and slid his arms under Jessica. She tensed for a second, but he whispered to her, and she settled against his chest. He lifted her into his arms and held her close.

When she'd walked out of the bathroom wearing his clothes, he wasn't prepared for the gut punch it would deliver. He'd given her the clothes, but seeing her in them awoke something primal and possessive inside him. He'd almost dragged her to his bedroom and claimed her as his right then and there, but he didn't ask her to come home with him so he could sleep with her. He asked her to come home with him because he wanted her safe. He needed to know she wasn't injured or in danger.

Holding her in his arms and carrying her limp body down the hallway to his bedroom brought that same primal feeling back to him. She was soft and warm and pressed tight against him, and he never wanted to let her go.

He didn't turn on any lights, and awkwardly kicked the covers back so he could set her on the bed and cover her up. As soon as she was on the mattress, she woke up, sitting upright so fast she almost collided with him.

"You're safe, Jessica. I just brought you to my room. It's Braden."

"Braden," she sighed. "I'm sorry."

"You don't have to be sorry. I just figured you'd be more comfortable in here than on the couch."

"I could have slept on the couch."

"I wanted you in here with me. If you're okay with that."

She nodded and laid back down, turning on her side to face the center of the bed.

Braden put his hand on her back, then went across the

hall to the bathroom. When he came back to his room, she hadn't moved, but he knew she was still awake.

Braden kept his tee and boxer briefs on as he slid between the covers and faced her. She looked up at him with tears glistening in her eyes.

"She's really gone, isn't she?"

He reached for her, pulling Jessica to his chest and wrapping his arms around her shaking body. "I'm so sorry."

She cried, her entire body trembling with each sob that broke his heart. He'd have given anything to take the pain from her. To bring Karli back. But he couldn't. All he could do was hold her.

When her sobs finally stopped, the snoring began. She'd cried herself to sleep. In his arms.

"Do you know where the girl is?" Damon asked the man standing in front of him.

Man was being generous. He was barely old enough to drink, but he was old enough to wield a weapon. He still had pimples on his face and greasy hair that said it hadn't been washed in far too long. Dark circles under his eyes made Damon wonder if he'd been sampling the product. Big mistake if he was.

"Someone picked her up," Silver said.

What the hell kind of name was Silver? Obviously, his parents didn't have high hopes for his future. "Who picked her up?"

Silver shrugged. "Don't know."

"Male, female? Was it the roommate? What were they driving? Which way did they go? Where was she when they picked her up?"

"It was a guy in a pickup truck. They went down the street. I don't know. She was at that store she went to the first night. Why do I have to tail the chick? I thought we wanted her alive."

"We do, which is why you're supposed to be following her. We need to make sure no one else hurts her. If she's dumb enough to be on the streets, she could easily be dumb enough to get caught up in the wrong spot and end up dead."

"And we want her alive?"

Damon swallowed his groan. Dealing with the next generation was a challenge to his sanity. What they were doing wasn't complicated. They were in the shipping business. And they had fronts in other companies so they could move everything without causing suspicion. The setup was borderline genius. And very effective.

But this one was a special kind of stupid. The kind that could cause more trouble than Damon was willing to deal with. Even if the fucker had value.

"We want her alive. You were instructed not to touch her."

"Yeah, yeah."

"Not yeah, yeah," Damon barked, slamming his hand on the desk.

That got the little shit to pay attention. He stood up straighter and avoided the direct eye contact he wasn't afraid of a minute ago. The fuck face needed to learn who he was talking to.

Silver was new, and still in a trial position, one the boss didn't know about. Damon recruited him when he realized his ex was living in Silver's building. It was easier to keep an eye on Raina when he had someone else helping out. Not that Silver knew that. He was as clueless as everyone else about what Damon was doing. All Silver knew was that he was supposed to kill Raina's roommate. Why wasn't important.

But Damon's plan to expose his ex and get her back hadn't worked so far. He didn't know where Raina was, even a week after her protector bitch friend was dead.

"Sorry, sir," Silver mumbled.

"We need this woman brought in to the police. Go to this address and find out if she's there. If she is, wait until she leaves in the morning, then call it in that you saw her leaving."

"Wait, why am I waiting if we want the police to find her?"

"Because I fucking said so," Damon growled.

"Yes, sir," Silver said quickly.

"I want you to follow her after she leaves. Make sure you don't lose sight of her. I need to know where she is and what she knows before she's arrested."

"Do you want me to interrogate her?"

"Don't talk to her. You're to watch her only."

"Yes, sir."

Damon stared at the man, waiting for him to leave. When he didn't, Damon shooed him. "Go. Now."

"Oh. Yes, sir. Thank you, sir." Silver bowed and hurried toward the door.

Damon rolled his eyes. If the whole thing went as planned, it would be a miracle.

There was a knock on the door almost as soon as it closed. Damon didn't bother calling out, he knew Mick would let himself in.

"Sir."

"If he fucks this up, kill him."

"Yes, sir. You have a visitor."

"Who?"

"A gift from the boss."

Damon grinned. "Let her in."

Mick stepped back and held the door open. The woman walked inside with zero hesitation. She paused when the door closed behind her, stopping where she stood and looking up at Damon with a sultry grin.

The women that came to see him were always instructed not to speak. It ruined it for him. They were the same. Dark hair, hazel eyes, curves he could sink his teeth into, and pussies ready to be fucked. Hard.

"Take off your clothes," he instructed the woman.

She didn't waste time doing what was asked. She lifted a breast and licked the peak of her nipple, flicking the edge with the tip of her tongue.

Damon dropped his pants and stroked himself. He sat on the edge of his desk, and she walked over to him, dropping to her knees in front of him. She parted her lips and sucked him inside.

He groaned and leaned in, holding her head in place while he fucked her mouth. She bobbed her head, taking him deeper and deeper with each stroke. Before he came, he pulled out, grabbing the condom she offered him and rolling it down his length while she stood and rested her forearms on his desk.

Damon lined up behind her and forced his way into her tight entrance. She was wet and ready. He slapped her hard, and she tightened around him. Her moan slipped out, not tolerated. He hit her again. "Don't make a fucking sound."

She nodded and pushed back against him. He grabbed her hips and let himself go, pumping hard and fast into her. When she reached between her thighs to stroke her clit, he slapped her again.

"You don't get to come, bitch."

She whimpered and put her hands back on the desk.

Damon gripped her hips so tight they sank into her flesh. She whimpered at the move, but he didn't care. She was only there to serve one purpose.

He grunted and thrust harder, his balls tightening. A few more strokes and his entire body went still, emptying out deep inside the woman.

When the aftershocks subsided, Damon pulled out of her. She whimpered at the loss. He tied up the end of the condom and tossed it in the trash under his desk. He had shit to do.

"Mick!" Damon called out.

The door opened and Mick's gaze went straight to the naked woman standing in front of Damon's desk. "Yeah, boss?"

"Get her out of here. You can have her if you want. She tried to come. Tell the boss not to send this whore back to me."

"Yes, sir," Mick said. He moved toward the woman.

Her eyes went wide. She turned back to Damon. "I thought—"

"You thought you were here to get fucked. You did. Now I'm done with you, and he gets a turn. Or he can kill you now."

She shook her head, her eyes brimming with tears. Mick grabbed her arm and yanked her toward the door, not letting her put her clothes back on before he shoved her out of the office and closed Damon's door behind them.

What the fuck was the boss thinking sending this one? He was surrounded by incompetent fucking assholes. And apparently working for one.

5

___

Jessica woke up instantly. She couldn't explain why, but all of a sudden, she was wide awake.

She didn't open her eyes, just listened to her surroundings. Then she heard a crash.

She jumped out of bed like it had been lit on fire around her. She stopped. Her reality rushed back like a tidal wave overtaking a beach, all at once with no compassion for the damage it was leaving behind.

Jessica grabbed the edge of the dresser, Braden's dresser, and gasped for breath. Panic gripped her, seizing every part of her body until her vision darkened around the edges and she thought she was going to pass out.

"Breathe, just breathe."

The voice was far away, but she heard it. It kept telling her to breathe, and her body obeyed it, sucking in air in gulps and choking it out when she forgot to exhale.

"Are you better?"

Jessica looked toward the voice and found Braden wrapped around her. She didn't know he was there.

"Better?" he repeated.

Jessica nodded.

"You were swaying when I walked in. I thought you were going to pass out," Braden explained as though Jessica had asked what happened.

"Sorry," she croaked.

"No need to be sorry. You've had a rough week. Did you sleep?"

Jessica nodded and let him help her to the bed. She sat on the edge. "Yeah. I didn't know I was so tired."

"I'm not sure how you got any sleep over the past week."

"I didn't. I guess that's why I crashed so hard last night. Thank you."

Braden nodded.

He studied her while she tried to breathe like a normal person. She couldn't look up at him, but she could feel his gaze on her.

"Are you hungry?" he asked after a minute.

"Yeah."

"I made breakfast. Waffles and eggs and sausage. And coffee."

That got her to look up. "Coffee?"

He grinned and reached for her hand. "I thought that might make you happy."

She let him pull her to her feet but didn't follow when he started for the door to the bedroom.

"Are you okay?"

She nodded, then stepped into him, wrapping her arms around him and holding him close. She couldn't say the words, but she wasn't sure she would have survived one more night if he hadn't shown up. She was a 'motel is roughing it' kind of woman. Camping, sleeping outdoors, God forbid a tent, were all things she never wanted to do. Having to do it because going to a hotel or motel could mean surrendering her life was that much worse. Especially alone.

"I'm glad you're safe," he whispered. His voice was thick with emotion, like he was struggling as much as she was.

She nodded against his chest, letting his warmth and comfort soak into her. She would be gone soon, and holding him for just a minute longer would make it slightly more bearable when she had no choice again.

"Let's have breakfast, and we'll go from there."

She tensed at his words. She wasn't prepared to fight him. She was too tired and worn out. But she didn't think he was going to be okay with what her plans were.

She had no choice but to leave.

The kitchen was tidy except for the dirty dishes from the breakfast he made. Waffles were piled high on the counter, scrambled eggs stayed warm on the stove, and sausage rested in a pan. It was domestic and pleasant and almost perfect. If it weren't all fiction.

Jessica accepted the plate he handed her and walked ahead of him to the food. She filled her plate with a waffle, a generous scoop of eggs, and a few pieces of perfectly browned sausage. She set her plate on the table and went back to the coffeepot.

Braden followed behind her every step of the way, repeating her moves in a way that irritated her for no reason at all. When they both sat down, he didn't say a word, just waited for her to take a bite before he did.

They ate in silence for a few minutes. The coffee finally penetrated Jessica's mind and brought her a little clarity. She ate slowly, not wanting to risk upsetting her stomach. But she was starving and couldn't deny how good it felt to be somewhere with a permanent roof and clean clothes.

"How are you feeling today?" Braden asked. He pushed his empty plate away and leaned back with his coffee mug.

Jessica shrugged. "Better. I really appreciate you letting me stay last night."

"You can stay as long as you want," Braden said.

Jessica took a breath and sat up straight. *And so it begins.* "We both know I can't stay. I shouldn't even be here now."

"Why not?"

"How many times have the police questioned you?"

His grumbled response was enough of an answer.

"I am grateful to you for finding me and giving me a good night's sleep and clean clothes and a shower, God I needed a shower, but I can't stay here any longer. The police will find me if I do."

"Then you should turn yourself in. Stop running."

Everything inside Jessica tightened. She expected him to say it, but it still surprised her. And it hurt. Braden was the kind of person who believed in the system. He was a part of it as a firefighter. But Jessica knew the system was flawed. She knew when someone was assumed guilty, it was almost impossible for them to get a fair chance. She was the one and only suspect in Karli's murder. The only person the police were looking for. They weren't considering that it could have been someone else.

"I can't," Jessica whispered.

"Why not? If you turn yourself in, the police will hear your side and realize you didn't do anything."

"No, they won't. They'll celebrate that they brought in a killer. They've already decided, and they've convinced the city, that I'm guilty. The only way this ends well for me is if I figure out who killed Karli and prove it to the police."

"How are you going to do that?"

Jessica shook her head slowly. Dark strands stuck to her lip. She swiped them away. "I don't know, but I have to try."

"Jessica..."

"Braden, no. Don't. I can't sit around and hope the cops figure out that I'm innocent. I saw the inside of my best friend's head. Her skull was squishy when I put my hand there to stop the bleeding. She was facedown on the floor and dead, Braden. She's dead. And instead of figuring out who killed her, the police are trying to find me."

"That's what I'm talking about. If you turned yourself in, they would have time to find the real killer. They would know you didn't do it."

"They won't believe me."

"You don't know that!"

"Did you? When you first heard about it, was your first instinct to trust that I was innocent? Or did you think, even for a second, that maybe I was guilty?"

Braden dropped his gaze to the table. "I'm not proud of that, Jessica."

Jessica didn't have a response for him.

"Taylor and Dex and Stacey and Wray all told me there was no way. They knew—"

"So four people had to convince you that I was innocent. I spent the night before Karli died in your bed! And you thought less than twenty-four hours later I could have smashed my best friend's skull in and watched her die."

"Jessica..."

She pushed to her feet. "It's fine, Braden. I get it. We don't know each other that well. We had one date. I thought it was a really good date, but we still don't really know each other. We see the world differently, and for me, that means I need to go because my future is on the line right now."

"Jessica..."

She pressed her lips up into a sad smile. She wasn't sure she'd ever see him again, and it hurt to imagine it could be the last time. But she had to do what was right for her and leave.

"Let me help you. Please. Just stay another night. Let me take care of you."

She shook her head, knowing that was the last thing she needed. Or wanted. Jessica had been responsible for herself most of her life. Her parents both worked full time, leaving Jessica and her younger sister home alone after school. Jessica helped Catherine with homework, then she would clean the house and cook dinner. Her parents did their best, but they relied heavily on Jessica. And she always rose to it. She wasn't going to back down now and let someone else take care of her. Not when she'd been taking care of herself since she turned eleven.

"Please, Jessica."

"I can't, Braden."

She didn't let him say anything else before she walked away. She went to his room and shoved her now clean clothes into the small bag she'd been using to carry her things. She looked inside and realized she was almost out of cash and even closer to being out of food. She didn't have a choice, though. She had to go.

"At least take some money," Braden said when she walked back into the kitchen with her sneakers and hoodie on. "You have to be getting low on cash."

Her pride told her not to take it, but her common sense stepped up and agreed. He stuffed a wad of bills into her hand and closed her fist around it.

"What about food? I have granola bars and stuff like that. I might have some MREs in my emergency kit. Let me go see."

He hurried to the garage, leaving the door open. Jessica considered ducking out the back door while he was out of the room, but she couldn't force herself to go just yet.

Braden ran back inside like he expected her to leave, sighing when he saw her standing in the same spot. He smiled sadly. "I know they're not that great, but it's an actual meal. It's better than trying to survive on junk food and granola bars."

Jessica nodded, her throat swelling with the emotions racing through her. She didn't want to go back out there, alone and cold and scared, but she didn't see another option. Staying with Braden meant relying on him, and she couldn't do that. It also meant risking his future. Harboring a fugitive wasn't something his bosses would likely overlook.

Not to mention he didn't see things the same way she did.

Braden walked across the kitchen and pulled her into his arms. He kissed the top of her head and held her to his chest. His body rose and fell with his breath.

Jessica struggled to keep her emotions inside. Her breath was shaky and uneven as she held on to Braden and gathered her strength. It would be nice to lean on him, to let him help her through everything, but she knew that wasn't the answer. She had to do it on her own.

"Are you sure you have to go?" Braden whispered.

Jessica pulled back slowly and nodded. "I do. I know you don't understand, but I have to do this. I have to find out who killed her. No one else is, but she deserves justice."

"I do get it. At least partly. I just wish it was different."

"Me, too."

Braden took a step toward her and lifted her chin slowly. Jessica let him, leaning in when he dipped his head toward hers. Their lips met in a gentle brush, a promise. His tongue touched hers lips, and she opened for him. A quick swipe of his tongue, and he pulled back to kiss her softly again.

It wasn't goodbye. It was just a kiss. A kiss that Jessica could hold on to when the nights were cold and lonely. It was a kiss that said there would be more. Eventually.

"Thank you," Jessica said.

Braden nodded. He walked with her to the backdoor, not questioning her when that was where she went. She zipped up her hoodie and pulled up the hood, hiding her black hair. She slid sunglasses on and slung the backpack loaded with food and cash over her shoulder.

"If you ever need anything…" Braden trailed off.

Jessica smiled at him and nodded. They both knew she wouldn't call him or return, but she appreciated the gesture. She waved, then turned and stepped off his deck.

The ground was soft from morning dew. Her sneakers would be soaked before long. She would have to look for newspapers to shove into them. A trick a woman shared with her on her second night to dry wet shoes.

Jessica looked around the yard, making sure no one was around. She walked straight back toward the trees that separated Braden's house from his neighbors. When she reached the trees, she looked back at the house.

Braden was still standing there, watching her.

Jessica pressed her lips up into a smile. It hurt to walk away from him. To have no idea when she might see him again. It wasn't fair. She lusted over him for years, her boss's younger brother always out of reach for her. But Taylor pushed, gently, and eventually Braden saw her.

When he asked her on a date, Jessica thought it was out of pity, but from the moment they sat down at the restaurant, it was like they were supposed to be together. They laughed and talked and connected in a way Jessica had never known.

And after their date, he asked her to come home with him. She'd never gone home with a man on the first date, but he wasn't a random man. He was Braden. He was safe and caring and everything she'd ever dreamed of. Jessica almost cried the first time he made her come, but then he thrust into her and she came a second time, and she knew she'd never get enough of him.

It wasn't fair to have that taken away. To have found him one day and lost him the next.

Jessica ducked behind a tree, going deeper into the barrier. Brush scratched at her clothes and tugged at her backpack. She moved slowly, not wanting to draw attention to herself. She crossed to the property next door and glanced back.

Braden was gone.

It stung, but it was for the best. She had no idea how long she'd be searching for Karli's killer. And Braden deserved to be with someone who was free.

Jessica kept moving, staying in the shadows of the trees. When she made it to a sidewalk, she turned in the direction of the city, walking with her head down so no one could see her face.

Braden strained to see Jessica, but she was well hidden in the trees. He hated that she had to leave. She would have been safer with him. Warm and fed and not alone.

Fuck.

Braden started to go after her when someone pounded

on his front door. His pulse kicked up. He glanced to where he last saw her, but she wasn't there.

The pounding came again, and Braden closed and locked his backdoor, then went to the front.

Two police officers were standing on his porch.

Braden crossed his arms. "Can I help you?"

"We received an anonymous tip that Jessica German was seen entering your residence."

"Really? Is this like the last time you came here and asked where she was?" Braden was about fucking done with the harassment.

"Mr. Wright, Ms. German is a suspect in a murder case. Hiding her from us is illegal," Officer Dickwad said. His real name was Maxwell, but Braden thought Dickwad was more appropriate for him.

"Seeing as I'm not hiding her, I don't think there's anything else we need to talk about," Braden said. He took a step back and started to close the door.

Officer Shitface, aka Dempsey, stepped forward and stuck his boot in the door. "Would you like us to bring you in for obstruction of justice?"

"Would you like me to break your fucking foot for being inside my home without permission? Do you have a warrant to search my property, gentlemen?"

Shitface and Dickwad exchanged a look. "We can get one," Dickwad said.

"Then I suggest you do that, because I do not give you permission to enter my home. I am not obstructing justice, and I am not hiding a murderer."

"Believing someone is innocent doesn't make them innocent, Mr. Wright," Officer Shitface said in his most condescending tone.

"And making up a timeline that doesn't match reality doesn't make them guilty."

"What are you talking about?" Officer Dickwad asked.

"I'm talking about doing your fucking job. Have you bothered to piece together a timeline yet? Because if you had, you'd see that Jessica called nine-one-one shortly after she arrived in the building, and that the person who reported seeing her leaving the building called it in while Jessica was still inside."

"Maybe she went back into the apartment because she left behind the murder weapon," Officer Shitface scoffed.

"You don't have the murder weapon?" Braden asked.

"You weren't supposed to tell him that," Dickwad barked. "We'll be back with a warrant, Mr. Wright. Until then, I suggest you check your sources."

"And I suggest you check yours, officers."

Braden glared at Shitface's foot. He finally removed it, right before Braden slammed the door.

"Fuck."

He rushed back to his backdoor and opened it again, hoping to see Jessica, but she was gone. It was better with a pair of cops around, but he still wanted to see her.

And wanted to know who reported her being at his house.

6

———

Braden waited for the elevator doors to open. He stepped out into the bland entryway that hid a lot more than it first appeared.

It wasn't long before Dex opened the secure door and waved Braden into the inner sanctum of F-BOMB. Braden followed Dex past a conference room full of arguing men and down the hallway to Dex's office. Dex closed the door and gestured to the lone guest chair while he took position behind his desk.

"I'm sorry to ask you for another favor," Braden said.

Dex waved his hand for Braden to hurry up and ask.

"I need to see the security footage from Karli's building."

Dex leaned back and crossed his arms over his chest. "What makes you think I have that?"

"You said you were trying to get it. I know English is good enough to have gotten it by now."

A ghost of a smile tilted Dex's lips up. Dex was the brains of the operation they ran, but English was the tech. Nine of them worked together to find, recover, and secure anyone and anything that threatened the border between the US and Canada. Former SEALs, most of them team-mates, first came together when one of them was kidnapped. The search brought the others to the area, and they decided to make it home.

Their lives tangled with Braden's when F-BOMB was brought in to find Wray when he went missing. The first time Braden asked Dex for a favor was when Taylor was in danger. Dex and Taylor falling for each other wasn't part of the plan, but Braden knew there wasn't a better person out there for his sister than the man on the other side of the desk.

"Why should I give it to you?" Dex asked.

"I found her. She spent the night at my house last night. She left this morning, even though I tried to talk her into staying, and within minutes, the cops were at my door."

"And?"

"I told you I thought she was innocent when you helped me find her the other day. I need proof."

Dex raised a brow. "You think the footage will provide that?"

Braden nodded. "I do."

"And you're going to share this with the police so they'll stop looking for her, or is this for you to prove she's innocent?"

"She didn't kill anyone. I know her. She wouldn't do it."

"Well, Taylor will be happy to hear you finally pulled your head out of your ass."

"Are you going to show me the footage?"

"There's nothing that will help. We've gone over it multiple times."

"Did you look at it in relation to the nine-one-one calls?"

Dex leaned forward, resting his palms on his desktop. To

most people, he would have looked calm, but Braden knew it was a position of power and danger.

"Jessica said she called nine-one-one." Braden leaned forward.

"I'm aware. I've heard it."

"She also said she was standing over Karli's body when she called. Which means—"

"Whoever called in that she was fleeing did it before she even arrived."

"Exactly."

"That's how they're framing her. Fuck." Dex jumped up from his chair and yanked the door open. He shouted down the hall for English, returning to his seat just before English walked in.

English nodded to Braden, then jerked his head toward Dex.

"We need to see the footage and the call logs. Time stamps for both."

English waved Dex to the side. Dex stood, surrendering his chair to English. English typed something into the computer and a minute later, sat back. "What are we looking for?"

"Jessica said she was looking at Karli when she made the call. We never looked at the timestamps for the cameras and calls together."

"Well, fuck me. That was stupid."

Dex nodded. He looked up at Braden and spun the screen. "Look at this. She enters the building at five-seventeen. The first call comes in at five-twenty-one. Jessica's call comes in at five-twenty-four."

"When does she leave?"

Dex skipped the video ahead and shook his head. "We

don't see her leave. She must have gone out a different door."

"But it still looks like someone called it in well before she left."

"Yep. Likely as she was walking down the hall or into the apartment. We haven't seen anyone else there who wasn't authorized. The building is secured, but it's common for residents to hold the door open for anyone coming in. There was a man leaving when Jessica arrived, and he held the door for her."

"Could it have been him?" Braden asked.

"Unfortunately, it could have been anyone. For it to be someone who described her the way they did, it's someone who saw her that day. Right then. Who knew what she looked like. She's there regularly, so it could be someone who recognized her, but it's more likely whoever called it in saw Jessica that day. Knew she'd be in the building and would be in the right apartment and hoped no one would pay attention to the timing."

"He was right," Braden said. "Whoever called it in was right. No one paid attention to the time. Just took what that nine-one-one operator said and rolled with it. Do we know she actually got another call?"

Dex nodded. "We heard it."

"Do we know anything about her? Could she be involved?"

English stepped forward. "Not likely. Mackenzie Chambers' college roommate was killed by her boyfriend. He tried to pin it on Mackenzie. She witnessed the friend's murder and called nine-one-one. The boyfriend called right after Mackenzie and said he saw Mackenzie kill the roommate. It was a definite he-said-she-said kind of thing, but the operator stood up for Mackenzie and helped her prove her innocence. They became good friends, and Mackenzie became a nine-one-one operator so she could help people at their worst moments. It sounded like this one hit her hard because it was a similar type of thing as her roommate, where the first person calls it in as a witness and the guilty one calls it in after. If Jessica was guilty."

"Which she's not," Braden growled.

"I get it. Dex has been drilling that into all of us for a week. Jessica isn't the kind of person I would point a finger at."

"So, who would?" Braden asked.

"That's the question. If you find out who pointed the finger at her, you find out who killed Karli."

"Jessica said Mackenzie called her by name. Said they had her name. Don't we know who called it in?"

"It was called in by a neighbor. Someone who said they were a concerned citizen."

"What does that mean?" Braden asked.

"It means they didn't give a name, and the phone wasn't a public registration," Dex said.

"I still don't know what that means," Braden said.

"It means the guy who called it in was using a burner phone," English provided. "I've run a trace on it and it's off. Chances are it was destroyed as soon as the call was made."

"Have you heard the call?"

English shook his head. "They have it buried. I can't get to it. The only thing we've been able to find is the number the call came from, but I can't get access to those calls. Jessica's call has been released."

Braden sighed. "Someone tipped the police off that Jessica was at my house today. Is there anyway to find out who did that?"

English's brows shot up, but he shook his head. "Those

tip lines don't track anything. They're anonymous so people can call without fear of retaliation."

"Shit."

"Well, the good thing is, we know for sure she's innocent. And we have the proof," English said.

"Do you think this will convince her to come in?" Dex asked.

Braden shook his head. "I don't know. She was pretty adamant that she had to keep looking for whoever is actually responsible."

"We can call Captain Patrick and make sure they know about this," Dex said.

"Thanks. I'd appreciate that."

"We can't promise anything, though. The department knows we have a connection to Jessica, so they've kept us out of this case. Captain Patrick isn't running the case. I'm not sure they'll take our evidence."

"It's not your evidence. It's just evidence," Braden argued.

Dex nodded. "True, but they have to uncover it on their own. And Jessica ran. That doesn't look good for her."

"If that nine-one-one operator hadn't accused her of killing her best friend, she wouldn't have run," Braden spat.

"I get it," Dex said calmly. "But it's not going to help Jessica. Right now, the best thing she can do is turn herself in and tell the truth."

"I agree."

"Do you have a way to reach her?" English asked.

Braden shook his head.

"Do you know where she's going?"

"She wouldn't tell me anything."

"Okay, makes sense. Well, there are some vacant houses in the city. I mean, we have a safe house on County Road, the big red house that's three-point-seven miles from the Fort Niagara State Park. If someone ended up all the way out there, I don't think anyone would find them for a long time. If it were me, I'd head to someplace like that. Especially with the technology we have set up in that house." English rubbed his jaw like he was just coming up with the idea.

Braden narrowed his gaze at English. Was he...?

"I'd go there, too. It's quiet, and the neighbors aren't nosy. Everyone keeps to themselves out there. No one would notice if the house was lit up at night or if someone was coming in and out. Plus, there's a big garage that would hide a large vehicle if I needed to drive out there." Dex shrugged.

Braden nodded slowly. Message received. "Thanks for your help, guys."

Dex and English shrugged. "Just sharing information that's already public knowledge."

Braden tilted his head in confusion.

"The nine-one-one call and the building footage have been playing on the news. Nothing new, but putting it together makes a difference," Dex said. "Hopefully Jessica finds a way to stay safe."

Braden smiled. "I hope so, too."

Dex stood and gestured for Braden to walk ahead of him. "Keep us posted on what's going on. And let us know if there's anything we can do for either of you."

Braden nodded. "Thanks. I mean it."

Dex nodded sharply. "Find her. Make sure she's safe."

"I will."

DAMON LOOKED up from his phone as the SUV rolled to a stop.

"Is this where you wanted to go, sir?" his driver asked.

Damon ignored him. He was new. Another new son-of-a-bitch that Damon had to deal with. Why the fuck was he getting all the new employees? He was too fucking important to be training the fuckwits. They needed to come to him understanding what they were expected to do.

Like not fucking question him.

Damon slid out of the vehicle. The vehicle was enough to draw attention, but in his pressed suit and wing-tipped shoes, there was no doubt everyone in the area would notice him.

Which was the point.

Damon looked around until he found a man watching him. Most of the people ignored him, but there were always some who saw the meal ticket. That was who Damon wanted to talk to.

Damon kept his gaze locked on the man as he made his way closer. It didn't take long before he moved toward Damon, as though the arrangement was already made.

The man stopped a few feet from Damon and looked him up and down. Damon's guess was he was in his thirties, but years of drugs and life on the streets made it tough to guess how old a lot of people were. "You got a job for me?"

Damon nodded. Having a network was valuable, more valuable than most realized. Damon was smarter than most, so his network was extensive. And loyal, because they knew the consequences if they turned on him, or thought about it. It didn't matter that the man in front of him was a stranger, he clearly knew who Damon was and what the expectation was.

"There's a woman hanging around. I need to know what

she knows about someone else." Damon showed the man a picture of Jessica.

The man licked his gums while he stared at the picture, then scanned Damon's suit. "What's in it for me?"

"Depends on what you find out. If you can tell me where her friend is, you can have it all." Damon opened the paper bag he carried with him to show the other man what was inside.

Drugs, food, and rolls of cash filled the bag nearly to the top. It was nothing to Damon, but it was everything to the greedy son-of-a-bitch who tried to snatch it.

Damon yanked the bag back and rolled the top back down. "Information first."

"How do you want me to get the information?"

"I don't care."

"I can rough her up?"

"As much as you want. Just find out where Raina is."

"Raina. Got it. When will you be back?"

"Tomorrow. Same time."

The man nodded eagerly, the promise of a fix already exciting him to the point of jitters. Or maybe it was the promise of beating on a woman. Damon didn't give a fuck as long as he found out where Raina was. Jessica was only important as a resource. But if she went on the run and ended up beaten or killed by a homeless drug addict, the truth would die with the stupid bitch.

"Do I get all of that?" the man asked as Damon turned around.

"If you find out where Raina is, you can have the entire bag."

"What if I don't?"

Damon glared at the man.

He nodded, his greasy hair falling into his face. He

bobbed his head and backed up toward where he came from. "Any chance I can get a little bonus pick-me-up?"

"Can't risk you not getting the information I need. Find out, then you can have it all."

"Yes, sir. I will. I'll see you tomorrow with a location on Raina."

"Good."

The man backed away, his clothes falling off his too-thin frame. The shoes on his feet were almost worn through. The drugs were likely the only thing keeping him alive.

Damon loved it. A man so desperate for a fix that he could barely function. That was all the intoxication Damon needed. He was creating a service, giving the people what they wanted. And people like that man wanted more and more drugs.

Damon got back into the SUV and tossed the bag onto the seat next to him. When the driver didn't move, Damon told him to go.

"Where are we going, sir?"

"Oh, for fuck's sake." Damon pointed his gun at the driver's head, letting him feel the cold metal against his temple. "I'm going to shoot you if you don't move your fucking ass. Now."

The guy nodded, the edge of the gun scraping the side of his head with each bob. He put the SUV in gear and took off, swinging around and pointing the vehicle back toward the office.

He was lucky. But he wouldn't be for long if he didn't figure out which end was his ass.

BRADEN DID NOT like the look of the park. It was one he'd been to more than once on night shift. It was large and public and home to many of the homeless. They'd built their own community there, with restaurants nearby who left food outside and plenty of places to sleep at night. And fire pits and grills to stay warm. All of which were lit when Braden arrived.

He parked his truck on the far side of the park, where it was dark and no one was hanging around. It was unlikely anyone would recognize him, but it was only a matter of time before someone got rowdy and a fire pit or grill was knocked over. Happened every year at this time. When residents were trying to squeeze the last little bit of summer from the park and the homeless were looking to use up the waste left behind.

Braden had been looking for Jessica since she left his house four days earlier. His two nights on shift were maddening, not being able to go out and search for her. Add to it the threats from the police department and his own chief about cooperating with the investigation or risking his future, and Braden was wound up tight and ready to attack anyone who pushed him too far.

Dex was still watching Jessica. Braden didn't ask how they were able to track her movements, but they were. And Dex told Braden Jessica was likely to be at the park.

Braden didn't rush through the park. Twilight had set in early and the fires made it hard to make out faces of the people hovering around the warmth. He didn't want to risk walking past Jessica and not see her.

He made it to the other side without spotting her. There were other places Dex said she could be. He turned to go back to his truck and check in with Dex when he heard someone shout from the tree line.

"Stop! Please!" a woman screamed, and everything inside Braden went cold. It was the kind of scream that was born of pure fear.

He took off running toward the sound, vaguely aware that he was the only one who seemed worried enough to help. The sound of flesh connecting turned his stomach.

Braden finally reached the woman, her black hair loose from the sweatshirt he'd seen her in four days earlier. A scrawny man held her by the back of the neck and punched her.

Everything inside Braden went cold.

Jessica.

7

———

"It's more fun when you fight," the scrawny man said, hovering above her. He swung again, connecting with Jessica's jaw.

She tried to bring her hands up to defend herself, but he caught her off-guard. The smells rolling off of him mixed with the fear inside of her, and she had to fight the vomit lifting up her throat.

"Get the fuck off her," another man growled.

Jessica was yanked forward as the new man tried to pull the skinny one off of her. Only when the new guy delivered a solid blow did the other one let go of her.

Jessica knew that didn't mean she was safe. It just meant the new guy wanted her more than the first one. She scrambled backward, trying to put distance between herself and the two men. The skinny one spun on the other one, feral and wild. He howled and swung, not connecting with the man who was more fit and mobile.

"Jessica, get out of here," the new man said, his gaze never leaving the man he faced.

"Braden?" The level of relief that swamped her weakened her knees. She wanted to cry.

"My truck is at the edge of the park. Go there. Now. I'll be right behind you."

"I need to find out where her friend is," the scrawny man shouted.

"Who is he talking about?" Braden asked.

"Raina," Jessica breathed. "He wants to know where Raina is."

"Karli's roommate?" Braden barked, his gaze flickering between Jessica and the man he held at arm's length.

"He grabbed me and said I needed to tell him where she is or he was going to kill me."

Braden shook the man, drawing his attention. Jessica wasn't sure how he hadn't passed out already. He was clearly high and most likely drunk, too, if the smell of alcohol on him was anything to go by.

"Why do you want to know where Raina is?" Braden growled.

"None of your business," the man snarled.

"It is if you're putting your hands on Jessica."

"He told me I could do whatever I wanted as long as I found out where Raina is."

"Who told you that?" Braden demanded.

The man's lips turned up and revealed crooked, stained teeth. He laughed, like Braden told him a joke. "I'm not telling you anything."

Braden dragged the man up close, lifting him effortlessly until his feet dangled above the ground. The smile on his face turned to fear when he realized he had no advantage. He tried to look down at the ground, but Braden shook him and forced his gaze back up.

"Who is he?"

"Put me down."

"Why? Are you going to tell me if I do?"

"No."

"Then why should I put you down?"

"I barely touched the whore. And she was asking for it, anyway. Walking about here like—"

Braden tossed the guy, his scrawny body landing beneath a large tree. "Don't you dare finish that fucking sentence. No woman is ever asking for it. Not unless she says the words, and even then, she always has the right to change her mind. The world will be a better place when you don't have any information to bring back to whoever tried to get you to beat it out of her."

Braden turned to Jessica as the man tried to scramble to his feet. Jessica didn't hesitate to go to Braden, letting him pull her against his side and hurry them away as the man chased them.

"No. You can't. He won't give me what he promised unless I can tell him where Raina is. He said Raina. Where is she? Tell me!"

Jessica practically had to jog to keep up with Braden. He kept his arm locked around her, his long strides eating up the ground between the man who tried to hurt her and Braden's truck. He pressed a button on his keys and the truck beeped in the dark night, a beacon for them.

Braden opened her door and lifted her up into the seat, locking the truck again after he closed her door. He paused, looking back where they'd come from, before he hurried around to the other side. He unlocked only his door, then climbed in and locked the doors again.

Braden cranked up the truck and took off, tearing away from the park like they were being chased. They were, but not by someone who could catch them.

He drove in silence for five minutes before he reached across the console for her hand. "Are you okay?"

Jessica was still shaking. She gripped his hand in hers and nodded.

"Fuck," he breathed. He yanked the wheel to the right and slammed the truck into park. "Come here."

He lifted her, bringing her body across the center console like she weighed the same as the man who attacked her. He held her close to his chest, his arms bracketed around her body, his warmth surrounding her like the last time he found her and rescued her.

Jessica shook and cried and pressed her nose to his neck. He smelled like Braden, like home. She tried to tell her brain she was safe and everything was okay, but the message didn't sink in until Braden whispered the words to her.

"I got you, Jessica. You're safe now. I'm not going to let anything else happen to you."

The tremors finally subsided, and Jessica's tears dried up. She pressed her hands to his chest, hiccuping as she tried to catch her breath. "I'm sorry."

"Why are you sorry? He attacked you. Fuck, Jessica, I'm scared, too."

"You don't seem like it." She lifted her head off his chest and looked down at him.

He brushed the hair from her face and smiled. "We can't both fall apart at the same time. Taylor taught me that. We have to take turns."

Jessica chuckled. "She says the same thing at work."

Braden's grin widened. "Of course she does."

"I'm sorry you got dragged into my mess again."

"Don't do that. Don't say it like any of this is your fault."

"But it is. If I didn't run—"

"You'd probably be in jail right now. I don't agree with it, but I am starting to understand it. Dex showed me the video. And the calls. There's no way you could have killed Karli. Someone saw you."

Jessica's sigh was so big, she collapsed onto his chest again. Knowing there was proof out there, proof that said she was innocent, gave her hope. She could go back to her life. Prove she didn't kill her best friend. People would know.

"The police don't believe it."

"What?" That wasn't possible.

"I told Dex what you said about being at Karli's when you called nine-one-one. We looked at the video, but the police don't believe it. Marcus isn't involved in the case because of his personal connection to you, so one of his lieutenants is running the investigation. The lieutenant said the evidence they have shows a different story. One that shows you leaving the building before the first call came in."

"That's not possible," Jessica breathed.

"I know. I believe you. But you're still in danger."

"That night... Raina's in danger, too. I went to Stacey that night. I told her she needed to get in touch with Raina. Do you think this could be her ex?"

Braden shook his head. "I don't know. Anything seems to be possible."

They sat for a minute, silent except for their breathing. Jessica became increasingly aware of the position she was in, her thighs spread wide over Braden's, his hands on her hips and hers on his chest. His cock thickened beneath her, his body recognizing their position at the same time as she did.

"I should..." Jessica said, shifting the same time Braden started to move her back to her seat.

"Sorry about that," Braden mumbled.

Jessica's cheeks burned in the dark interior of the truck.

She didn't feel the least bit attractive or desirable, but Braden didn't seem to mind.

"Um, where are we going? I don't know if we should go to your house again."

Braden shook his head. "No. The cops showed up right after you left last week."

"What?"

"Someone tipped them off. They were on my doorstep before you were even out of sight."

"Oh, my God."

"They've been watching me, and I'm guessing they have someone on my house at all times."

"Did they follow you here?"

"No. I made sure of it. But they know what I drive, so we need to go somewhere with a garage. Somewhere off the grid. With tech we can use where no one will find us."

"Um, yeah, I don't know anyplace like that. I'm not a spy."

"Do you trust me?" he asked.

Jessica didn't have to think about the answer. She knew it with every inch of herself, from the moment they met. She always trusted him, even when he was just her boss's little brother and not the man she was having a hard time not falling in love with.

"Of course," she whispered.

"I'm going with you."

"Braden, you can't. You can't put your career and your future in jeopardy."

"If my career is in jeopardy because I'm helping you solve the murder of your best friend, maybe it's not the right career for me."

"Braden—"

"I'm not leaving you alone. Not after what just

happened. Dex and English mentioned a place. We can go there."

"They mentioned a place?" Jessica asked.

Braden chuckled. "Yeah. They were trying to help. It'll be safe. I promise."

"Okay. Let's go."

BRADEN COULDN'T STOP LOOKING at Jessica on the drive to the house English and Dex mentioned. He wasn't positive where it was, but when he saw the big red house, he knew it was the right place.

His suspicions were confirmed when the huge garage opened as he pulled up to it. He closed the door behind his truck and shrugged. "I guess someone was expecting us."

"I just hope it isn't the police," Jessica mumbled.

Braden nodded. He wouldn't admit it, but he hoped the same.

They got out of the truck and made their way into the house. It was a big house but had an older, tired look. It was not the kind of place that would draw attention, but the little touches most people wouldn't notice were definitely there for security.

"There's food in the fridge," Jessica said in wonder.

Braden walked over and saw the fridge stocked with all kinds of things. Fresh fruit frand vegetables, milk, cheese, and plenty of meat. He opened the freezer and found the same, including a container of Jessica's favorite ice cream.

"How in the world...?"

"Taylor and Dex," Braden answered. "They had to know we were coming. I worked the last few days, but I've been in touch with Dex. I asked today if he knew where you were. They must have figured we would end up here."

"And you're sure it's safe."

Braden nodded. "Absolutely."

Jessica took a deep breath, her chest rising sharply before falling again. She bent at the waist and hugged herself, then she collapsed onto the floor.

Braden rushed to her, hating that she was going through all of this. He didn't know a more caring person than Jessica, and for anyone to think she was capable of hurting someone pissed him off.

For him to have thought it pissed him off.

He sat on the floor and wrapped his body around hers. He pulled her into his arms and held her, rocking her and whispering that she was safe until she quieted.

"I keep doing that to you. I'm so sorry." She sniffed and started to pull away.

"Doing what?"

"Falling apart."

"If you didn't fall apart, I'd wonder what was wrong with you."

"Yeah, but I keep doing it to you. Every time I see you."

"And are you seeing anyone else?" Braden's tone held a bit of an edge. He didn't mean for it to, but the question held a double meaning for him. They only had one date and talked about a second, but he didn't know if Jessica was dating anyone else. If the night they spent together was as big of a deal for her as it had been for him.

He hadn't been able to think about anyone but Jessica since that night, and not just because she was in danger. He kept rushing in to protect her, to help her, but he had no idea if he was just one of many and she was ready to be rid of him.

"No," she said softly. "I'm not seeing anyone else. In whatever way you need an answer to that question. I wasn't dating anyone else before our date, and I haven't had contact with anyone else I know since I touched the back of my friend's skull. There's been no one except you, Braden."

He pulled her in again and kissed the top of her head. "I'm sorry. I didn't mean to make you defend yourself."

"It's okay."

"You're going through enough, Jessica. I have no right to be questioning you. Why don't you go take a shower or a bath or maybe you're hungry? I don't know. I'm sorry. I just don't want to fuck this up."

"You're not. We're in an impossible situation. We had one date, a great date, and everything is on hold now. It has to be. I'd never ask you to stand by me through all of this. We're barely dating. And I can't put this on you or Taylor or anyone else."

"We're here for you, Jessica. We want to be here for you. Taylor has been doing what she can. She's had Dex and his team watching you the whole time. They've always known where you were—"

"What?"

"She couldn't stand the thought of you being alone and of anything happening to you. She knew you wouldn't accept help, and Dex's team was required to turn you in if they officially found you, but Taylor needed to know you were at least okay. And me—"

"You're putting everything on the line right now, Braden."

"I'm off for a few days. I just worked, and now I'm off for a week. I don't need to explain where I go when I'm on my days off. No one needs to know."

"But you're harboring a fugitive."

"No, I'm staying at a friend's house."

Jessica snorted.

"What do you want to do first? Shower or eat?"

Her stomach growled. She looked up at him sheepishly. "My stomach says food, but I'm not sure I can tolerate the way I smell much longer. I was seriously considering a jump in the River."

"The Niagara River?"

"Desperate times."

"Go shower. I'll make dinner. Any preferences?"

"If it wasn't wrapped in cellophane and could have been sold in a vending machine, it'll be better than anything I've had since I last saw you."

Braden smiled through the stabbing pain in his heart. Jessica deserved better. He wasn't going to stop until she had it.

She walked down the short hallway toward what he assumed were bathrooms and bedrooms, and Braden turned to the kitchen once again. It was well stocked with just about everything they could need.

Something like chili sounded good, but he didn't have time to make that. Maybe for the next night. For tonight, he was going to rely on old favorites. Comfort food. Fried chicken, macaroni and cheese, and roasted broccoli.

Braden got to work, losing himself in the process. By the time Jessica came back, smelling like lavender and honey, everything was done and his stomach was growling for more than the food. Jessica's hair was wet and hung in clumps around her face. She wore no makeup and was dressed in clothes she must have found somewhere in the rest of the house. And she was stunning.

Even with the beginning of a black eye.

"I didn't notice that before. Are you okay?"

She touched her cheek and nodded. "It hurts, but it'll heal."

"I'm sorry I didn't get there sooner."

"You can't protect me all the time, Braden."

But I want to whispered through his head, shocking him into silence. He didn't know where the thought came from, but it was the truth.

"I am happy you showed up when you did. I don't know what I would have done," Jessica continued, taking his silence as agreement.

"I'm glad you didn't have to find out." The words came out rough, choked out of him as if by force.

She nodded. "Dinner smells amazing."

"You smell amazing."

She breathed a laugh. "Much better than before. If it wouldn't remind me of being on the run, I might have to buy more of that body wash."

Braden couldn't stop himself from crossing the room to her and pulling her into his arms. He found himself itching to touch her whenever she wasn't right there with him. And after the emotional upheaval of her life, he wanted her in his arms even more.

He pressed his nose to the side of her head and inhaled deep. The shampoo and body wash tickled his nose, but beneath it all was Jessica. The woman he still smelled on his sheets. The one he wanted back in his bed.

Jessica held on to him, sighing after a minute. Her body relaxed into his, her full breasts tight against his chest. They swayed together, unconsciously, letting the quiet and the peace of the safe house sink in.

They were safe. She was safe. And he was going to do everything in his power to make sure that didn't change ever again.

8

———

Jessica hated leaning on Braden. It rubbed her in all the wrong ways. But she couldn't deny that having him there made her feel safe and protected in ways she'd never been.

Her family wasn't horrible, but she never felt like she made sense with them. Her parents were high school sweethearts, and they struggled to build a life together. They worked long hours and saved as much as they could in hopes they could retire one day. Her sister followed in their footsteps, marrying her high school sweetheart and building a life in the same small, dying town where their parents lived.

Jessica was the only one who wanted more. Who wanted a life outside their small town, in a city with excitement and anonymity and people who wouldn't pry into her past.

Until she was accused of murder.

She was comfortable being alone, but being alone with everything hanging over her was hard. Being alone when she went about her days and nights was simple. She had friends and coworkers and she went out and went on dates, but nothing went too deep. Karli was the closest friend she'd ever had, and there was a lot about Jessica Karli never knew. And never would now.

Jessica had never felt so alone in her life. With Karli gone, she'd lost her best friend. That had to be why leaning on Braden was so appealing. Because it was someone. Karli normally would have been the person Jessica turned to if she needed something, but without Karli...

She hated to think about it. It still turned her stomach. When she closed her eyes, Jessica could see the back of Karli's head. The only thing she was grateful for was that her hair covered her face. If Jessica had to look into her dead best friend's eyes... She couldn't even imagine.

"Do you want to eat?" Braden whispered, breaking the spell Jessica let herself fall into. A spell that said she was okay, instead of whispering that danger was everywhere.

Jessica nodded and pulled out of his embrace. He gestured for her to get food first. She couldn't bring herself to shy away from filling her plate. Not when it made her mouth water and her stomach rumble like she hadn't eaten a proper meal in months instead of the few days since he last cooked for her.

It was still a long time to go without proper food. Jessica was never the kind of woman who hid from her figure, and working for Taylor at Birds of a Feather, where plus size women were celebrated instead of shunned, Jessica grew confident in who she was. When Taylor ordered in lunch, it was always more than enough and no one thought twice about getting extra if they were still hungry. Taylor built a world where women of all shapes and sizes were told they belonged.

Jessica hated that she'd never go back to that world.

Even if she could prove her innocence, and even if Taylor would consider letting her back, Jessica wouldn't be able to show her face there again. Not when her coworkers wouldn't trust her. Not when they might wonder if she could have been guilty.

Jessica hadn't figured out where she would go when everything was over, but she already knew she'd leave Niagara Falls. Her best friend was gone, her job wouldn't be the same, and she had no one and nothing else to keep her there. It only made sense.

"I'm sorry I didn't have better news for you," Braden said when they sat at the table.

Jessica shrugged, trying not to be upset by it. She'd been neck deep in fear and grief for ten days. She was almost to the point of being numb. "I'm not surprised. If it was that easy to prove, they wouldn't still be trying to find me."

"Someone must have manipulated the video."

"I guess. I just wish I knew who was doing all of this."

"Me, too. But we'll figure it out."

"When do you have to go back to work?"

Braden flinched at the subject change. "Next week. Why?"

"I'm just wondering what's going to happen after that. I don't even know if I should stay here."

"You're staying here. We both are. I don't even want to think about what would have happened with that man if I hadn't gotten there when I did."

Jessica didn't either, but she knew she never would have gone with him willingly. Or given him any information. Not that she had any. She had no idea where Raina was. "Why do you think he wanted to know where Raina is?"

"I don't know. It makes sense that her ex is trying to find

her. Do you know anyone else who would be looking for her?"

"No. Just him. She said he's bad news."

"Why would he go after you?"

"Maybe her ex is the one who's behind all of this. That was my first thought. That's why I went to Stacey that first night. When Raina left Shelter in the Storm, she moved in with Karli. Stacey said when people leave, if they stay in the area, they usually go back to their abuser if they don't have a support system in place. Karli offered Raina her extra bedroom so she had a safe place to live. But if her ex found out, he might have tried to find out where Raina was before he killed Karli."

Braden shook his head. "The news said there was no evidence of any other trauma. Karli's only injury was the skull fracture. She didn't have defensive wounds either, so they don't think she knew her attacker was there."

"I don't know if that makes it better or worse," Jessica admitted. "I'd like to think Karli would have fought back, but then she would have had to face whoever killed her. Look him in the eyes and know why he was there." Jessica shivered.

"Yeah, but then she'd have DNA on her body from the attacker and there'd be no question about your innocence."

"I just want to find her killer. I know I'm innocent, but I want to find out who was willing to steal someone so amazing from the world."

Braden reached for Jessica's hand as a tear streaked down her cheek. She didn't bother brushing it away as another one followed right behind it. She stared at her food, wondering if the grief would ever go away.

Jessica eventually picked up her fork and ate her dinner.

It was amazing, as expected, and she went back for more macaroni and cheese. When she was so stuffed she was sure she couldn't outrun another bad guy, she waddled to the couch and sat down.

"Do you feel better?" Braden asked when he joined her a minute later.

"I do. Thank you for feeding me again."

"I'm glad I can do something. I feel like I'm not helping you at all."

"You don't have to put yourself at risk. You shouldn't. This is my fight."

"I'm not letting you fight it alone. We're going to figure out who killed Karli, clear your name, and get justice for her."

Jessica forced a smile and nodded. She hoped it was possible.

BRADEN SUGGESTED A MOVIE, and Jessica agreed. There was a part of her that just wanted sleep, but she knew it wouldn't come. A movie was a good distraction. Almost as good as the man holding her hand on the couch.

When the movie ended, Braden asked if she wanted to get some sleep. It was well past dark, getting close to midnight, and Jessica could feel the weakness settling into her body. She nodded and followed him down the short hallway.

The house had three bedrooms. All three rooms had queen beds and private bathrooms. Jessica used the bathroom in the first bedroom earlier when she showered, and pilfered clothes from the dresser in the corner so she had something clean to wear.

"Which room?" Braden asked, stopping when he realized there were three.

"I used this one earlier. I can sleep in here." Jessica didn't want to assume Braden was looking to share a room and a bed again. She wasn't opposed, but she wasn't going to force herself on him.

"Do you want to sleep alone?" Braden asked, his voice softening, as though he was afraid of her answer.

"Not really. But I—"

"Thank Christ," Braden breathed, interrupting her unnecessary argument.

Jessica exhaled a laugh. Braden followed her into the bedroom, closing the door behind them. She walked to the bed and sat tentatively on the edge. "I hate this."

"Me, too. But we're safe here. No one knows we're here. And I was watching to make sure we weren't followed."

"I wish I understood why someone decided I should take the fall for Karli's death. Why they thought I would do something like that."

"Whoever did it saw an opportunity. It wasn't personal."

"It sure feels personal."

Braden nodded. "Are you going to be able to sleep here?"

"I'm going to try. I can use another room if you're worried I'll keep you up."

He shook his head and moved toward her. He sat down next to her on the edge of the bed and took her hand in his. "I will sit up with you all night if you want. I just want you to be okay."

"I'll be okay when I figure out who killed my best friend."

Braden pulled her against his side and held her.

"I don't know what I'm going to do without her. I don't know where I'm going to go."

"What do you mean?"

"I can't stay here."

"In this house or in Niagara Falls?" Braden's voice was tight.

"Both. People don't forget things. Even if I can prove I'm innocent, there are going to be people who think I'm guilty. I won't risk Taylor's company or anyone else I know getting dragged down by all of this."

"Does Taylor know you're thinking this?"

Jessica laughed mirthlessly. "I'm sure my accounts have been frozen, and my apartment is a crime scene. Or under surveillance or whatever. I have no doubt they've been through Birds of a Feather, too. After everything with your dad... I won't do that to Taylor. She's been too good to me to consider trying to go back there. When it's safe, I'll send her my official resignation."

"She won't accept it."

"She won't have a choice."

"Jessica, you can't run from this. You have to fight to prove your innocence."

"I am! God, Braden, I am. But it's exhausting. I've been sleeping on benches and sitting upright under trees. I've walked so many miles I wonder why I haven't lost a dress size or two. I'm tired and hungry and scared all the time. And if I somehow find a way to prove the video the police say is true is actually not true, and if I find a way to convince the police not to press charges for me running, and if I am finally proven innocent, I'm still guilty in the eyes of the people here. No one believes I didn't kill Karli."

"I do. Taylor does. Dex and his team do. And Marcus and Frannie and Stacey and everyone at Birds. You have people on your side, Jessica."

She inhaled a deep breath and blew it out slowly. She

wanted to believe he was telling the truth, but it was hard after the hell she'd been through. Not just seeing Karli dead, but the threats and the danger of being on the street. There were homeless people who lived together in a community of sorts, but Jessica was an outsider. She wasn't welcome. She was alone. Usually she liked that, but being alone out of necessity was different from out of choice.

Braden could list all the people who were on her side, but none of them could do anything. She'd never be free unless she found out who actually killed Karli. And even if she did figure that out, there was no guarantee Jessica would be free. People said things all the time. Things they didn't mean. At the end of it all, Jessica knew she only had herself to rely on.

"Don't shut me out," Braden whispered. "I'm here because I want to be. I don't want you to run. I want you to fight."

"I am. And I will. But I can't just sit back and let you fight my battles for me like you did tonight."

Braden sighed heavily and nodded. "I know. And I'd never ask you to."

"Thank you."

He squeezed her hand and rubbed his thumb along her skin. The move was soothing, a soft comfort after almost two weeks of harshness. Jessica became aware of Braden all of a sudden. They'd been sitting together, talking, but as silence settled between them, everything else settled around them.

The desire and care she'd been fighting since the day she met him filled the room. She still remembered the first time he walked into Birds of a Feather. He was in uniform, walking toward Taylor's office with purpose. Taylor mentioned her brother was coming to check out the office, but Jessica didn't realize he was a firefighter. It was her first week on the job after Taylor convinced her to work at Birds of a Feather. They'd known each other for years, but Taylor never opened up about anything.

Jessica stared at Braden that day, so mesmerized by the casual grace he carried himself with. She was so drawn to him that she didn't notice the glass door she was walking toward and smashed right into it.

Her coffee cup flattened in her hand and exploded all over her. It was everywhere from her hair to her shoes. She was mortified, but Braden didn't even see her. He was oblivious.

And now, he was holding her hand, and the woman who fell for him on sight knew he'd be the one regret of her life. The one person she'd hate herself for walking away from. It had to happen, but until then, she wanted to grab hold of every last bit of living she could get.

"Braden," she whispered. She couldn't force more words out. She wanted to ask him to kiss her and touch her and give her a night she'd never forget, but Jessica was comfortable in the background. She didn't like the spotlight. Even if there was only one other person in the room.

"Jessica," he answered, his voice equally rough. The edges of it skidded over all her sensitive parts and lit her up.

"Please."

His free hand came up and cupped her jaw. She rubbed against him like she'd been starved for attention. His fingers dove into her hair and turned her face toward his as he lowered his mouth to hers.

She opened for him before their lips met and found him seeking her just as eagerly. She whimpered, and he groaned. His fingers tightened in her hair, tugging the strands and tilting her head where he wanted it to be.

Jessica needed this. She needed him. To be able to let go and know he would take care of her. For just a little while. She wouldn't give up control forever, but for now, it was exactly what she needed.

He'd never know how she really felt about him. That she'd loved him forever. But that didn't matter in the moment. All that mattered was his lips on hers, his hands on her body, and letting go.

Braden leaned over her, forcing her body to the bed. He still held her hand, an intimacy Jessica wasn't sure he was even aware of, but one that grounded her. He wasn't there for sex. It wasn't primal and without feelings. It was two people who connected, who shared one night together, then had any chance of more ripped away from them. They were getting a second chance. It wasn't going to last, but for one night...

"Jesus, Jessica," Braden groaned, tearing his lips from hers. He kissed his way across her cheek, licking and sucking on her tender pulse point before nipping at her jaw.

Jessica forced her breath in and out, drawing his scent in deeper with each inhale. She pushed away all thoughts of everything going on outside the room they were in and focused on Braden and his magical tongue already driving her crazy without even removing any clothes.

"Oh, God," Jessica whimpered. "Yes."

He reached the edge of her shirt and stopped. His erection dug into her side, telling her he was as ready as she was, but he stopped.

"Are you sure you want to do this?" he asked.

Jessica nearly cried. She wanted him more than she wanted anything in the world, and he wasn't sure.

"If you don't want—"

"God, I do, Jessica. More than you know. But you're alone

and vulnerable and scared, and I feel like I'm an asshole who's kidnapped you and is forcing myself on you. I don't want you to think you have no choice here."

"If I have a choice, then I want you inside me, Braden. Please."

9

———

BRADEN HAD TO STOP HIMSELF FROM TACKLING HER WHEN SHE said she wanted him inside her. Fucking hell. She had no idea what she did to him. He was turned inside out. But he wasn't going to rush or make her feel anything less than desirable.

Braden closed the distance he put between them, not caring about his erection against her thigh and only wanting another taste of her. She wrapped her arms around him and held on tight as he licked into her mouth and groaned.

He couldn't remember the last time he'd been so hard. The last time he waited so long to be with a woman. Casual sex had lost some of its appeal lately. He wasn't looking to settle down, but he wasn't interested in one-night stands or flings with women he'd never see again. But he never saw Jessica coming.

Their first date was unlike any Braden had ever been on, and when he couldn't stop smiling and laughing, he knew he would regret it if he didn't invite Jessica back to his place. When she said yes, he accepted that they were crossing a line they couldn't uncross. Their lives were already tangled together, and to make that knot even tighter by sleeping together was a risk Braden wasn't known for taking.

But she was irresistible, and he jumped in with both feet.

Lying on the bed next to her in the safe house pushed beyond any risk Braden had ever taken. He didn't like risk, even though his job made it seem otherwise. In a fire, there were no ulterior motivations or manipulations. Fires were created to destroy things.

People were the opposite. People could take anything and twist it into whatever they needed to make themselves feel better. Braden had no patience for deceit. Not after the way he was raised.

Jessica was different. That's why he was so drawn to her. She was strong and independent. She didn't ask him for anything. But for the first time in his life, Braden wanted to give everything he had to another person. To Jessica.

She whimpered, shifting her hips toward him, her center seeking his. Braden put a hand on her hip to still her movement and eased his body on top of hers. She spread her thighs for him without hesitation, letting him in. His cock pulsed with excitement, knowing exactly what was coming.

Braden trailed his fingertips down her neck to the edge of the borrowed shirt she wore. He followed the curve of her breast over the soft cotton until he found her tight nipple. He rasped his fingers over it, making her gasp and thrust up against him.

He kept moving his hands lower until he met warm, soft skin again. He spread his hand wide on her side, lifting the edge of the shirt. She wiggled under him, and he moved back.

As soon as his weight lifted off her, she reached for the

shirt and tore it off. Then she reached for him and brought him back down to her. She wrapped her legs around his hips and spread her hands across his back.

Braden pumped against her, needing the friction against his cock. He wasn't sure how long he was going to last once he got inside her, but until then, he was determined to make her forget about everything going on.

"Braden," she cried.

He didn't know what she wanted, but he knew he wanted to give her everything. He leaned back and yanked his shirt off, then kissed his way from her lips to her navel. He circled her belly button with his tongue and fought her legs as they tried to wrap around him again. When he tugged at her pants, she finally released her thighs and helped him to shove her pants and panties to the floor.

Braden couldn't take his time getting to her sweet center. He pressed her thighs wide with his hands, then hooked her ankles over his shoulders so she stayed spread out for him. He leaned in, inhaling deep as he drew closer to her, and sucked hard on her without any preamble.

She screamed and bucked against his face. A moan followed right behind the scream, then her hips moved with his tongue. Seeking him, searching for her release, demanding everything he had to give.

He was happy to deliver for her. To hear her mumbled noises and feel her channel tighten when he slid a finger into her. He curled his finger and teased her spot. She went still, then moaned again.

He licked and sucked on her until her breaths became pants and her noises became nothing more than soundless whispers. He thrust a second finger into her and sucked hard on her clit, and she let go of the orgasm she was fighting.

"Oh, God. Braden. Fuck, yes!" Her shouts were all the motivation he needed to keep going. He backed off just enough to trick her body into starting to come down, then went full in again, relentlessly flicking her clit with his tongue until she begged him to make her come.

"Please. God, please. Oh, yes. Yes. Yes!"

His cock strained against his pants. He was going to come soon, and he realized he didn't have any condoms.

"Fuck!"

"That's what I'm hoping for," Jessica said, her smile sex-drunk and satisfied. She reached for him. "I still want to feel you inside me."

"I don't have any condoms."

"Oh," she said, the fog clearing from her gaze. "Um..."

"Let me see if there are any in the bathroom," Braden said, already on his feet and hurrying that way. He yanked open the drawers in the cabinet, cursing when one after another proved useless. He pulled the doors open and nearly fell to his knees when he saw an unopened box of condoms.

He yanked the box open and grabbed a sleeve. He wasn't going to stop again. He ripped one package as he walked back to Jessica and shoved his pants to his ankles, stepping out of them on his way.

"Did you find one?"

"I found a box." He rolled the condom on, hissing from the contact.

"Thank God," she murmured.

"I agree." Braden crawled up the bed to where Jessica had moved to. He positioned himself between her thighs and whispered, "Now, where were we?"

"We were about to get to the good part."

"Are you saying that last part wasn't any good?"

"Oh, no. It was amazing. But I like feeling you inside me."

"I want to feel you come when I'm inside you," Braden whispered. His throat tightened. Sex was always a balance. She comes, then he comes. One each, most of the time. But with Jessica, it was like everything else. It was different. He didn't want to stop watching her come. He wanted to see it and feel it over and over again. And he wanted her body clenching around his when he went over the edge.

"I want that, too," Jessica said, her voice as whispery as his.

Braden kissed her nose, then kissed her lips. He couldn't believe he ever doubted her innocence. She was strong and smart and amazing. And she was innocent. And he was going to do everything in his power to prove it so he could convince her to stay in Niagara Falls and stay with him.

Jessica shifted under him as he moved to line them up. Her heat welcomed him in, her body slick and ready for him. He eased in slowly, enjoying the feel of her body stretching for him with each gentle thrust. Then he got past her resistance and sank all the way into her, and they both groaned.

"Oh, God," Jessica mumbled.

"So good," Braden said.

He stayed deep inside her for a minute, then she wiggled to get him going. He withdrew, then stroked into her slowly, the drag of their bodies resisting separation, then welcoming his intrusion. He felt his orgasm building by the second stroke into her, and he worried he'd go off before she did.

"Braden," she whimpered.

"God, Jessica."

"Please. Harder. I'm—"

He slammed into her.

"Oh, fuck!" she moaned. "Yes, more. Please. Braden!"

Her body tightened around him, sucking him in and refusing to let him back out. He fought her for one more stroke, pouring everything into it and letting go when he hit the depths of her body. "Jessica!"

Every inch of him tightened, then released. He felt the orgasm all the way to his toes with a sharp tingle that was like fireworks going off along all his nerves. He jerked and throbbed and emptied into her, then collapsed on top of her.

It took a few minutes for Braden to come back down to earth and realize he was still lying on top of Jessica. He made a move to roll off her, but she resisted. Only for a second. When she let him move, he missed the feel of her body immediately.

Braden rolled out of bed and got rid of the condom. When he came back out of the bathroom, Jessica was waiting to go in. He didn't know what he was supposed to do. Should he wait for her? Lay on the bed? Get dressed?

He decided to go back to the bed and leave his clothes on the floor. If she wanted to get dressed, he would, too, but he usually slept naked, anyway.

Jessica came out and looked at the floor where his clothes were. Her lips turned up when she saw they were still there, and she walked right to the bed and crawled under the covers with him.

He pulled her against his side and kissed her head. "You're amazing."

"I think that was definitely both of us."

"Not just that. How strong you are and how beautiful you are and how smart you are. I really hope you change your mind about leaving Niagara Falls after all of this is over."

Her breath hitched, and he wondered what it meant. She didn't explain, just nuzzled against his side and whispered, "Thank you."

TEN DAYS. It had been ten days since Karli died. Ten days since Jessica left her life behind and stopped thinking about the future. And then Braden Wright fought his way back into her world.

Jessica listened to his breathing even out and slow and tried to calm her own racing heart. She hadn't been able to think about anything beyond Karli for the past ten days. Not even the date she had eleven days ago with Braden.

But now... It was all she could think about. She replayed every moment of the night in her mind. She wanted to believe Braden meant what she thought he meant when he said he hoped she would stay. Her Braden-Wright-loving heart said he felt the same and wanted to marry her and have babies with her and grow old with her. But the rational, realistic part of her—ahem, everything else—said he wasn't even close to going there.

Did he say something during their date that said he was interested in her like that? Jessica went into the date thinking he only asked her out as a favor to Taylor and left the date wondering if she'd ever find another man who made her forget about Braden Wright. She wasn't thinking forever that night. Only because she knew he wasn't.

But did she miss something?

A forever with someone else was always a dream. To find

a man who made her feel like her parents felt about each other, like her sister felt about her husband. Jessica didn't find that in high school like the rest of them, so she thought she was broken, that something was wrong with her. She figured she'd find it in college, but that didn't happen either. She was thirty-three and still had no inkling of that forever feeling.

At least, not one she thought was returned.

But could she have been wrong about Braden the whole time? Was it possible he was thinking the same thing she was?

Jessica asked herself the question over and over until she made herself crazy. She wasn't the forever girl anyone wanted. She was the one who stayed in the background and made sure things got done. She wasn't the star. Braden Wright deserved a woman who was.

A woman who was younger and healthier, like him. A woman who stood out in a crowd. A woman who matched him in every way.

Braden rolled over and reached for her, his arm tightening around her waist. He kissed her shoulder. He slid his other arm under her head and pulled her body tight to his. An erection poked against her backside. "Jessica," he whispered in his sleep.

Her heart cracked wide open. If she wasn't already gone, that would have done it. Instead, all that did was give her hope she wasn't sure she'd ever be able to reach out and grab on to. Before she could try, she had to find a killer.

"What did you find?" Damon demanded.

Silver stood in front of him, again looking like he'd been sampling the product. "Someone's been there since I left."

"No shit. The friend and a shit ton of police."

"Yeah, but I mean someone else. There were things missing. Clothes and stuff."

"How do you know that?"

"You said to look around. There were empty drawers and hangers. It looked like someone packed for a trip."

"What about mail?"

Silver shook his head, the greasy strands falling over his shoulders.

"Did you find anything that tells me where she is?"

"There was a piece of paper on the counter with a phone number."

"What was the number?"

Silver read it off his phone.

Damon didn't have to look up the number. He knew what it was for. He'd been keeping an eye on the business since they opened their doors. The business, and the business owner.

Shelter in the Storm.

"I don't know what it's for, but it looked like it might be important."

"I'll figure it out. Anything else?"

"Nah, man, the place was pretty dead. No pun intended." Silver chuckled at his joke, slapping his hands together.

"Where's the other one now?"

"I don't know."

"You were supposed to be following her. You've had an entire day to figure out where she went since she left the park."

"Yeah, man, but no one seems to know where she is. That dude you had rough her up up and died this morning. I was going to ask him, but the cops were all over the park. No one wants to talk about anything. They think they're going to be next when they see a guy like you and me roll up."

Damon raised a brow and scanned the man standing in front of him. Their only similarities were that they were standing in the same room. Silver's ratty jeans and band tee told the world he was a low-class individual with zero style. His glassy gaze screamed of a man who'd used one too many drugs in his life, probably in that day. And the scrawny figure he thought looked tough was characteristic of the same bad habit that allowed him to be brought into Damon's world in the first place.

Damon was better than Silver in every way. His clothes were custom made. Everything about him spoke of money. He stayed away from drugs he sold, mostly, and he made sure he could take out any potential threat against himself or the Company. Damon's reputation was earned the hard way. Through years of proving himself.

And he was finally being rewarded, even if the rewards were coming from an incompetent boss who only succeeded because of Damon.

"I'm sure people see us exactly the same," Damon said without emotion.

Silver smirked and nodded. "Damn straight. Hey, that other woman you're spending all this time and energy trying to find. Who is she?"

"None of your fucking business."

"Well, she sort of is. I mean, I killed her roommate because you wanted to get to her. I told the police that other chick killed the roommate. I'm sneaking into her place because you want to know where she ended up. I have her— I mean, I got a right to know who she is. Ya know?"

"You have her what?"

"Nothing, man, nothing. I ain't got nothing."

Damon leveled the sniveling scum with a look that would have made him piss himself if he had any sense. When he didn't, Damon decided he'd let the son-of-a-bitch live just a little longer.

"Since you've been so helpful, I think I can use your help again. Come back to see me in a week. By then, I'll have more information for you."

"You got anymore product you need me to move until then?" Silver asked hopefully.

Damon looked the man up and down. He shifted his feet and scratched his nails along his palms. He avoided Damon's gaze.

"Not today," Damon said. "But if the next job I give you goes off without a hitch, I'll give you a bonus. Free of charge."

Silver's eyes lit up. "Like, a product bonus?"

Damon nodded. "Just for your enjoyment."

"Yeah, man, yeah, I'll make sure everything is good. No problem. A week?"

"One week from today."

"I'll be here. Thanks, Damon!"

Silver let himself out of the office like they were equals. Damon turned his neck until it cracked, then twisted it the other way. Snot-nosed son-of-a-bitch had no idea the hell he would be in if he was actually in the Company.

10

Braden used the phone in the safe house to check his messages. He couldn't get texts without turning on his phone, which was not a good idea, but he wanted to at least listen to any voicemails.

"Wright, what the hell is wrong with you? You know you're not supposed to be unavailable. The police came by the station looking for you. Said you hadn't been home. You better show up to work as planned. That vacation you asked for? It's been denied. Since you aren't supposed to not be here. You need to show up to work on Saturday or don't come back at all. You got me?"

Braden closed his eyes and groaned. Taking off was a risk he was willing to take, but he didn't think the police would figure it out so quickly. Not when his schedule was never consistent. He thought he'd have at least a few days before the police started questioning his whereabouts.

The message his chief left was from the day before, which meant the cops were up someone's ass at the fire station on his first day off. And Braden only had two more days before he had to report in, since his vacation was now canceled.

The only other message Braden had was from Dex asking how the bratwurst was from lunch the other day and if he needed anything to go with it. Braden was beyond confused.

"Is everything okay?" Jessica asked, walking into the office behind him.

They spent their first full day in the safe house learning what was there and where everything was. They searched the other bedrooms and bathrooms, discovering a box of condoms in each bathroom, and they found the office off the living room, complete with more technology than either of them knew how to use.

"I don't really know. Dex left me a voicemail about bratwurst."

Jessica snorted. "That's clever."

"You understand?"

Jessica tilted her head, letting her dark hair fall to the side. She tucked it behind her ear and narrowed her brows. "Bratwurst? German? My last name? I'm guessing he was asking something about me."

Braden shook his head. "I never even thought about that. How did you know?"

"One of my sister's friends in high school called her bratwurst."

"Are you sure they were a friend?"

Jessica laughed. "Yeah. The friend's last name was Mayer, so she was hot dog."

"People are weird in the Midwest."

"Yes, yes, we are. What did the message say?"

Braden dialed his voicemail again. He skipped past the

voicemail from his boss and put the phone on speaker when Dex's voice came on. Jessica listened with a faint smile.

"Do you have a way to get in touch with him?"

"I can call him, I guess. I'd think the phone can make calls."

"Do you think it's a good idea?"

"Only one way to find out. What do you want me to say?"

"If he answers, tell him what's going on. I'm assuming he left that voicemail because someone is likely listening to your messages. Or he thinks they could be."

"When did you get so smart about this stuff?" Braden teased.

"When I had to ditch my phone and go on the run for killing my best friend."

Braden crossed the room to her in two large steps, not hesitating before he pulled her into his arms. They spent the last two days with only each other to talk to, and Braden was not hating it. Jessica was funny and smart and creative. She was also passionate and fun. He hated the idea of having to go back to the real world as much as he craved being able to live a life with her after this hell.

Jessica wrapped her arms around him and held on. She didn't say anything, but he could feel her tension. When it finally melted away, he leaned back and waited until she looked up at him.

"I'm sorry. I shouldn't have said that."

She shrugged. "It's my reality. I want to believe it isn't, but it is. I hope one day I can have a life where I don't have to worry about being picked up by the police, but I'm not there yet."

"You will be." Braden kissed her softly, loving that after two days of living together, she didn't hesitate to meet his lips halfway. "Are you ready to call Dex?"

Jessica nodded.

Braden held her to his side as he walked back to the desk. He dialed Dex's number from the list next to the phone. Convenient.

"Hamilton," Dex said.

"Are you busy?" Braden asked.

"Not too busy for you. How are you?"

"As good as can be expected."

"Good. Happy to hear that."

"The bratwurst is good, too," Jessica said.

Dex chuckled. "That's good news."

"Have there been any updates?" Braden asked.

"Unfortunately, nothing helpful."

"Shit."

"How's Taylor?" Jessica asked.

"Rallying the troops. She's started a social media campaign about people falsely accused of crimes."

"Oh, no. She can't lose her business because of me. People are going to hate her," Jessica cried.

"Business is better than ever," Dex said calmly. "And even if it wasn't, Taylor wouldn't stop. She believes in you. We all do."

"Too bad the cops don't. The video they have..."

"I know. I tried to get them to see reason. Marcus believes me, but he's not on the case because of his connection to you. It's too risky."

"I understand. I just can't believe someone did this. To Karli and to me."

"We're going to find out who," Dex promised.

"Do you have a way of getting me some footage? There was a man leaving the building when I was walking in. He held the door for me. Maybe if you can find him, he can confirm what time I got there."

"We saw him, but I couldn't make out his face. Maybe you'll recognize him from another day since you know what he looks like. You can access our systems. It should be easy to find whatever you need. Is there anything else you need?"

"No, but thanks. I really appreciate the support," Jessica said.

She turned to leave the office, but Braden held back. He lifted the receiver to his ear. "I'll be right there," he told Jessica. She nodded and left the room. "You still there?" Braden asked Dex.

"Yeah. What's going on?"

"It sounds like I'm almost out of time."

"I figured that would happen."

"I had a message that said my vacation was not approved. And asking where I am."

"What are you going to do?"

"I can't leave her, but if I don't go back, they're going to come after me. It'll be harder for us to hide together."

"Especially when the cops are trying to put pressure on us to turn over everything we have."

"They're what?" Braden barked.

"Lieutenant Juarez is doing his job, and he's good, but that means he's not ignoring things. He knows we work closely with Captain Patrick, and he knows about my relationship with Jessica, so he thinks we know more than we're letting on."

"Which means what?"

"Which means they're going to do everything they can to find a reason to force us to give up anything and everything."

"Can't you just tell them you don't know anything?"

"We already tried that."

"Shit."

"Yeah. I would recommend you find a way to get back to work and don't step out of line or they're going to come after you even harder."

"How do I do that?"

"You have to follow the rules, Braden. That's not usually an issue for you."

"I've never had someone like Jessica in a situation like this. I know running was the wrong thing to do, but I get why she did it. She's innocent, Dex. She didn't kill her best friend. And if she's caught, they're going to throw her in jail and never find Karli's actual killer."

"They aren't looking anyway."

"And you think it'll be better when they have her in custody?" Braden spat.

"No, I don't. But I also know you throwing away your future isn't going to help her."

"What would you do if this was Taylor?" Braden asked.

"Are you sure you want to compare? Because I'd die for your sister. I'd give anything for her. She's the love of my life. If you're saying Jessica is the same, then I'm all for it, but if you're not sure, don't even go there, Braden." Dex's voice was rough and harsh, angry.

"I wasn't trying... I don't know what I'm saying."

"Figure it out before Jessica hears you saying shit like that. She's already being put through hell. Don't make it worse by toying with her feelings. She deserves better than that," Dex lectured.

"I'm not toying with her."

Dex didn't reply for a full minute, long enough for Braden to squirm and hate that he started the conversation.

"Get back for your shift," Dex said in parting.

"Yeah, I—"

Dex already hung up.

Braden sighed and set the phone down. Dex wasn't entirely wrong, but Dex also didn't know the situation Braden and Jessica were in. It was different than anything else. It was the two of them against the world, and Braden was determined to win.

He just hoped winning didn't mean losing, too.

JESSICA SPENT the rest of the night reviewing footage from the day Karli died and the few days before and after. The cameras in the lobby didn't catch the man's face the day she saw him, like Dex said. Jessica remembered looking at him and smiling, but she couldn't picture his face. He was Black with short hair and a light gray suit. She tried to find other footage of him, but there was none for the rest of that day or the next. She didn't even see footage of him walking into the building.

The chances of finding the man were becoming smaller and smaller. If she could find him, Dex might have something he could go to the police with so they could question him, but until she found the man, she couldn't clear her name.

She kept going through the footage. The building was busy that day. Jessica tried to look for anyone who could have killed Karli, but she didn't know what a killer looked like. The whole thing would have been so much easier if she did.

Braden fixed them dinner, then he coaxed her away from the computer with a movie and ice cream. Her mind stayed on the video footage, but she was stuck.

The next day, Jessica wanted to get back into the

computer, but she stupidly decided to turn on the news while she was drinking her coffee.

The top story was her, and not just that the police were still looking, but that one of her coworkers thought she was guilty.

Ramona Wilder sat on a couch in the studio talking to the blonde anchorwomen.

"You've known Jessica German for how long?" the anchorwoman, Brenda, asked.

"Two years. We work together," Ramona said in her high-pitched nasal tone. Jessica found her irritating, but Taylor hired her because she came highly recommended by a former colleague.

"And you believe she's capable of doing this?"

"Absolutely. We work for a clothing company, and Jessica tore into a mannequin once. She stabbed it with scissors and slashed at it. She was insane."

"Wow. That sounds unnecessarily aggressive. Did you know the victim?"

Ramona shook her head. "No, I didn't. But I heard her name a few times. Jessica didn't seem too happy one night when they were getting together. She said she didn't want to go. Why would you ever say that about your best friend?"

"Did you see Ms. German the day of the murder?"

"No, thank God. She might have killed me, too. But I saw her the day before. She was uptight and anxious. Snapping at everyone in the office. Someone invited her to go out for a drink with a few of us, but she blew us off and claimed she had plans. I guess she was getting everything ready to kill her supposed best friend."

"I see there's no love lost between you and Ms. German. Be careful."

"The police will find her. She's not that smart. If she's still on the run, she must have had help. There's no way she could have avoided the police for so long. She's not very street smart."

"Well, good to know. Maybe that'll help the police bring her in. We want our community to be safe. And getting someone like Ms. German into custody would make all of us feel better. Thank you for your time today, Ms. Wilder."

"Thank you for having me, Brenda."

Jessica fought the urge to throw her coffee mug against the wall. How dare she! Ramona didn't know the first thing about Jessica, and she was on the TV telling the whole city that Jessica was dangerous and could have killed someone.

"Hey," Braden said sleepily.

Jessica growled.

"Whoa. What's going on?"

"Ramona was just on the news. Telling everyone how horrible I am and that I'm not smart enough to have avoided the police, and that she knows I killed Karli. That bitch doesn't know a thing about me. God, what is wrong with people?"

"They want their ten minutes. I'm sure Taylor will take care of it."

"Taylor shouldn't have to. Taylor has a business to run. She shouldn't be worrying about all of this. God, Ramona has been a pain in my ass since the day she was hired."

"What does she do?"

"She's an assistant. I think she wants my job."

"Taylor will see right through that."

"It doesn't matter. I can't let Taylor go down because of me. She worked too hard to risk her company."

"What are you going to do?"

"The same thing I set out to do when I walked out of

Karli's building that day. Find out who killed my friend and put an end to this."

"Are you any closer to figuring that out?"

Jessica sighed. "No. I can't find that man anywhere on the cameras."

"Is there another entrance for residents?"

"Yeah, but there aren't any cameras there."

"That doesn't seem safe."

"They have to have a keycard to get in that way, but it's also an emergency exit. It's how I got out that day."

"I wonder if Dex can pull those records. Leaving isn't the issue."

Jessica stopped, listening for a faint noise that was new. She tilted her head, realizing the sound was coming from the office. "Is that a phone?"

Braden walked with her to the office and hit the speaker button on the ringing phone.

"Pick up, pick up, pick up," Taylor whispered.

"Taylor?" Jessica asked.

"Oh, my God, you're there. Jessica, do not watch the news. Channel five. Just don't."

"I already saw it," Jessica admitted.

"Are you talking about that Ramona woman?" Braden asked.

"I've already fired her for the things she said. She's no longer a part of Birds of a Feather."

"Taylor, you can't do that," Jessica said.

"Yes, I can. It's my company, and HR was supportive of me making that decision. She went on TV and slandered your name. That's not legal."

"She didn't say anything that wasn't true."

"Except that she thought you could be capable of murder."

"That's her opinion. Taylor, she can sue you for wrongful termination."

"It'll be worth it. Jessica, you're like a sister to me. I always thought of you as the closest thing I had to a friend, but after I met Dex, my life has opened up. I don't want to be the uptight bitch I used to be, and that means getting close to people. I know you. I trust you. You're one of my favorite people in the world, and anyone who would go on TV and say those things about you is not someone I can trust. Ramona got a severance package. She'll be fine. But I'm not willing to have someone working for me who would do something like that. I made that very clear to the rest of the staff, and all of them are in agreement with me. We're all behind you, Jessica."

Jessica sucked in a breath and tried not to cry. She'd felt so alone, like it was just her against the world, but she never was. She had Taylor and the rest of her coworkers, and Braden, Dex and his team. She wasn't going to stop fighting for her freedom until she got it.

"Thank you," Jessica whispered.

Braden hugged her to his side and kissed the top of her head. "Thanks, Tay-tay. It means a lot to know you're out there fighting."

"I am not giving up. We're looking for everything we can. I know it's not easy right now, but we're with you. Both of you. Braden, when you get home, let me know. I think I'm being watched, but I'm not willing to leave Jessica alone."

"When you get home?" Jessica asked.

"Back to work. Did you not tell Jessica you had to be back at work tomorrow?" Taylor asked.

Jessica looked up at Braden. He hung his head. His eyes were closed. He ran his free hand over his head.

"I thought you had the week off," Jessica said.

"They denied his vacation," Taylor provided.

"Bye, Tay-tay," Braden said, pushing a button to end the call even as Taylor protested.

"What's going on?" Jessica demanded. She pulled out of his embrace and crossed her arms over her chest. Just as she was feeling like she could do this, something else changed.

"I got a call from work. If I don't show up tomorrow, they're going to fire me."

"What the hell? Why didn't you tell me?"

"Because I know you're going to argue with me."

"No, I'm not. You need to go back to work."

"I know. And I want you to come with me."

Jessica drew back like he slapped her. "No." She turned and walked out of the room. He was right. She was definitely going to argue.

11

Braden expected it. Hell, he told her she was going to fight him on it. But it still bothered him.

He watched her retreat and drew a deep breath. Getting angry at her was not going to help convince her to leave the safe house and turn herself in. He wasn't sure anything would, but he was going to try.

He followed her out of the office a minute later. She was in the kitchen like nothing happened, making breakfast.

"Jessica," he started.

She waved the butter knife she was holding at him. "No. Don't even start this. I told you I didn't want to go back. I can't."

"The police—"

"Are going to throw me in jail and shout from the rooftops that they caught a killer. And Karli's actual killer is going to kick his feet up and laugh."

"But—"

"Nuh uh, Braden Wright. Don't you dare try to argue with me about the system and how we need to trust it. I don't want to hear it. The system is why I'm here in the first place. If that nine-one-one operator hadn't accused me of killing my best friend, I would have stayed in that room with her dead body and talked to the police. She is the reason I ran. And I know it isn't fair to blame her for my actions, but that scared the hell out of me. I brought Karli pizza, for fuck's sake. I was supposed to be there to tell her about our—"

Braden cocked his head to the side. It was the second time she cut herself off from telling him why she was at Karli's. There was something about the way her cheeks turned pink and she avoided his gaze, suddenly so focused on the bread she was putting in the toaster, that clued him in to what the conversation was going to be about.

He moved around the edge of the peninsula. She backed up as he did. Her legs were bare under the shorts she must have pulled on when she left him in bed earlier. The only thing she slept in was his arms, which he was not hating at all. The tee she wore slid off one shoulder, showing him the side of her neck and the top curve of her breast. Her hair was a mess, and she was flushed and trying not to smile, and Braden swore he'd never seen anyone more beautiful in his life.

That was the moment he knew he loved her. The realization made his step falter, but he shoved it down and moved toward her.

"Braden," she warned.

He didn't care. She swung the butter knife at him as she chuckled and tried to escape him. He boxed her in.

"What did you go to Karli's to talk about?" he asked.

"Nothing," she said, her cheeks darkening with the lie.

"I don't believe you. I think you went to tell her how our date was. Were you going to tell her how we kissed like teenagers in the parking lot? Or about how I couldn't keep my hands off you when we finally made it back to my house? Or about how many times I made you come before we fucked so hard I nearly blacked out?"

"You did?" she gasped, meeting his gaze.

He was right in front of her. He cupped her jaw with one hand and brushed his thumb over her racing pulse point. "I'm hard right now just thinking about that first time with you. I hated Wray for calling me and dragging me out of bed. I wanted to spend the day with you. Talking to you and kissing you and making you come again and again and again."

He whispered the last part in her ear, then licked the shell. She trembled against him, dropping the butter knife with a clang to the floor before leaning against him and pulling him in close.

"Braden," she whispered.

He knew that whispered plea now. He understood what it meant. Instead of denying her what they both wanted and needed, he lifted her onto the edge of the counter and fitted himself between her thighs.

His cock notched against her warmth, and he kissed her like he hadn't tasted her since that first night. She whimpered at the sudden, forceful intrusion, then gave it right back to him with the thrashing of her tongue against his.

He pulled her body to the edge of the counter and pressed his cock to her center, letting her use him to get herself off. He fucked her right back, the friction of their clothes only spurring him on as she lost control.

"I want to feel you. Please."

He pulled back from her and tugged at her shorts. She lifted one side of her butt, then the other, helping him to pull her shorts off. She gasped at the cold countertops beneath her bare flesh.

He dropped to his knees and pushed her thighs wide. She was so wet she was almost dripping onto the counter. He leaned in and licked her, capturing her juices before he captured her clit.

"Braden!"

He wrapped his arms around her hips and pulled her forward. She leaned back, supporting herself on her hands as he held her on the very edge, literally and figuratively.

"Oh, God," she whispered. "Please. Yes."

Her body pumped in shallow thrusts as he licked and sucked her clit. Her breathing turned ragged, and her words lost all meaning as she raced closer to her orgasm. He felt her losing control and went with her, sucking hard on her clit and sending her over the edge and into oblivion.

She screamed and cried and fucked his face as she came. He licked her softly, knowing he wouldn't last through another orgasm like that. He wanted to be inside her.

Jessica put her hand on his cheek and lifted his face. He stood, kissing her and letting her taste herself on him. She moaned and held him close, wrapping her legs around his body.

"Condom," she murmured when she pulled back. "Please tell me you have one."

"I'll be right back," he said, running to the bathroom. He shoved his pants down and left them where they fell, then rolled the condom on during his race back to her. She hadn't moved.

"Please," she said. Her fingers were lazily stroking her clit, and Braden nearly collapsed at the sight of it.

"Fuck me," he groaned.

"That's the plan," she said, reaching for him with the same hand she was just using on herself.

"Touch yourself while I'm inside you."

She looked up at him, vulnerability in her gaze. He waited until she nodded, and his entire body swelled. She trusted him.

He positioned himself between her thighs and eased inside her. They moaned together when he was fully seated, then again when he withdrew to thrust into her hard.

"Oh, God," she moaned, her fingers dipping between her thighs.

Braden looked down, his body flushing with heat when he watched his cock disappear inside, her just beneath her fingers. Her short nails scraped against her clit, then retreated for her fingertips to fly over the tight nub. He held her thighs, unable to pull his gaze from between her legs.

"Braden," she whimpered.

He was right there with her. He let go and fucked her hard, pumping his hips as fast as he could. His balls slapped the edge of the counter, but he didn't care. He was inside Jessica. He was watching her touch herself. They were both rushing toward orgasms that might make him pass out, but he wasn't about to miss one damn second until then.

"Jessica," he grunted.

"Oh, God. Oh, God. Yes. Yes. I'm coming. Yes!" she shouted.

Her body locked around his and pulled him in deeper. He fought her as his cock demanded just one more hard stroke. He slammed into her, and everything shook with the powerful release. Her hand was trapped between them as his body poured into hers, a shout echoing out of him like he couldn't hold anything back from her.

Braden stood there, praying he wouldn't pass out, letting the pulsing and tremors stop before he pulled back. Jessica looked up at him with glassy, smiling eyes and freshly fucked, flushed cheeks.

"How does it get better every time?"

He leaned down and kissed her. "I think it's you."

She shook her head. "I've never experienced this before. It must be you."

"You make me feel everything. Watching you was the sexiest damn thing I've ever seen."

"I've never done that in front of anyone. I didn't even realize I was until you said something."

Braden kissed her hard. "You can touch yourself in front of me any time you want. It was hot as fuck."

"Right back at you."

He grinned and finally moved back. He helped her hop down from the counter with a smile. He disposed of the condom in the kitchen trash while Jessica used the bathroom.

Braden picked up her shorts and panties and met her outside the door, where he'd left his bottoms. He was pulling them on when she peeked out of the door.

"I've seen it before. You can walk around here naked."

Her cheeks pinked again. "It's just weird."

"I'd rather you walk around naked. We can both walk around naked."

"Until you leave," she said. Dropping her gaze.

Braden forgot about their argument. And about needing to leave the next day. He wanted to stay there with her forever. To protect her and make sure she was safe. He didn't want to leave. But he had no choice.

"I'll let you get dressed," he said, handing over her bottoms. He walked to the kitchen and picked up the butter knife she'd dropped earlier. He put it in the dishwasher and rested his hands on the counter. The scent of their sex was in the air. He needed to clean the countertop, but he wasn't sure if it was the last time he'd be inside Jessica and he needed to savor it for just a little longer.

She came up behind him, but he didn't move. She ran her hand up his back. Affectionate. Loving. He turned and pulled her into his arms.

"I fucking hate this," he admitted.

"Me, too."

"I believe in the system. I know it works. But I get why you aren't sure about coming back with me."

"The system works when it isn't rigged. For some reason, it's rigged against me. I don't know why. Someone wants me to take the fall for this. And the so-called witness is being protected by the police. They haven't released his name or anything. The only reason we know about him is because the operator told me."

"They must have a statement from him. Something more than the call."

Jessica shrugged. "I don't know. If they do, I haven't seen it."

"That can set you free."

"Not if he's lying. If he's part of all of this, the police are going to believe him and not me. Which, so far, is exactly what's going on."

Braden sighed. "This isn't fair. You shouldn't be dealing with this."

"There are a lot of people who are accused of crimes they never committed. And a lot of them never have a chance to prove their innocence."

"You're not coming with me, are you?"

Jessica shook her head. "I can't. Not when I know they'll never listen to my side of things."

"I don't like it."

"I know."

Braden held her, refusing to let go. They had twenty-four more hours together. Maybe they could find something. Something that would allow her to leave with him. Something that would prove she was innocent.

It wasn't much, but it was the only hope he had.

DAMON WATCHED the footage from the camera he installed in the hallway outside Silver's apartment. It was how he found Silver in the first place. He hadn't bothered to go over the footage in weeks since Raina wasn't there, but Silver's behavior said there was a reason.

Silver unlocked the door with the key Damon gave him weeks earlier. He glanced up and down the hallway, then walked inside, closing the door behind himself.

Damon sped through the time when no one was in the hallway. He wanted a camera inside the unit, but he didn't have a way to get inside and place one. Not without it being suspicious. He hoped the one in the hallway would be enough. So far, it had been.

Silver reappeared, and Damon returned the video to normal speed. Silver looked at the camera, then the other way down the hall. He locked the door, but just before he walked away, he dropped something. Something that he didn't have when he went into the unit.

Damon growled. He jumped the video backward to see what Silver had. It was small, the size of an envelope. When it fell, it didn't float, so it was definitely heavy. But Damon couldn't tell what it was.

He lifted the receiver on his desk and waited until someone picked up. "Yes, sir."

"I need Silver here. Now."

Damon didn't wait for an answer. He slammed the phone down and replayed the video. Again and again and again until Silver finally arrived.

"What did you take from the apartment?"

"Uh, what apartment, dude?"

Damon stood and spun the computer around. He hit the spacebar to play the video and stared at Silver as he watched himself leaving Raina's apartment.

"Uh, that was, uh, nothing, man. I mean, it was just sitting there. No one missed it."

"What. Was. It?"

"There was this little box thing in the bedroom. It had some cheap jewelry in it. Nothing expensive. I left the box. I just put the stuff in an empty envelope."

"How do you know it was cheap?" Damon demanded. Every word out of Silver's mouth served to make Damon more and more angry. He knew what the answer was, but he needed to hear the stupid piece-of-shit say it.

"I just guessed?"

"You guessed? You didn't try to sell any of that jewelry to a pawnshop?"

Silver shuffled his feet and looked at the floor.

Damon slammed his hand on the desk. "Do you have any idea how many cops frequent pawnshops looking for stolen items? And you just brought a bunch of stuff to one? I told you to go in there and look around. What the fuck were you thinking?"

"I didn't think it would be a problem. The chick's dead, and the other one is gone. I mean, who was going to miss anything?"

"Where's the jewelry?" Damon asked. His voice was low and harsh. Anger boiled in his blood. His fingers itched to rip Silver's fucking head off and stomp on his skull.

"It's in my apartment."

"And you really think that's a good idea? To have evidence from the apartment across the hall inside your place?"

"The police already talked to me. They got my statement and all that. They're too dumb to think the person who called nine-one-one might be the person who killed the chick."

Damon closed his eyes and took a breath. The man was an idiot. If there was any other option, he'd already be dead. But he was useful since he wasn't actually an employee of the Company. The boss had no idea Silver existed, or that Damon was using him to get to his ex.

"Since you didn't follow orders, I have a new assignment for you. You need to go to Shelter in the Storm and bring Raina to me."

"How in the hell am I supposed to do that?" Silver balked.

Damon shrugged. He tugged the sleeves of his shirt down and smoothed out his suit. "I don't know, and I don't care. Get it done. And don't fuck up this time."

"How did I fuck up last time?"

Damon had enough of the back-talk and got up in Silver's face. He had a good four inches on the slimy scum of a man. Being up close allowed Damon to smell the odor emanating from Silver. Not a pleasant one. "You lost the bitch we framed for murder, which means she's out there figuring shit out. With help. You took something that didn't belong to you, making it easier for the cops to figure out you're the one who killed the roommate. Raina is mine. I want her back. If you harm her or lay one hand on her, it'll be the last thing you fucking do. Now, find her, bring her here, and I won't have to kill you for being a waste."

Silver swallowed and nodded. He wisely kept his mouth shut. He backed up, not turning around until he opened the door and left.

Damon stared at the door and seethed. He hated involving others. Especially when he couldn't trust them. But he had no choice. Raina was his, and he was going to get her back, but Damon knew better than to be seen anywhere near Shelter in the Storm.

12

———

Jessica watched the sun brighten on the other side of the curtains. It looked like the day was going to be beautiful. Sunny and happy and completely opposite of how she felt inside.

Braden was leaving.

Jessica knew he had no choice. He needed to go back to work. He'd be charged as an accessory or something if he stayed with her. His career would be over.

But she hated knowing she'd be alone again.

It was nice to have a few days where she was safe and warm and not alone. To have Braden to hold her every night and talk things through. After spending most of her life alone, having someone there was new and different and good in all the ways she thought it would be bad.

Except he was leaving.

Braden stirred next to her and reached over. Even in his sleep, his warm hands found her body. He shifted closer to her and kissed her shoulder, waking up slowly. "Are you awake?" he whispered.

"Yeah."

"Did you sleep at all?"

"Yeah, I'm good," she lied.

"You were only up before me once since we got here and you jumped out of bed right away. Do you really think I'm going to believe you?"

She breathed a laugh she didn't feel and snuggled against his body. He inhaled deep, pulling her closer.

"I don't want to leave you."

"You have no choice."

"We always have a choice," he said.

Jessica shook her head. "You can't, Braden. You love your job. You can't just quit."

"None of this is fair."

"People deal with this all the time. People who look like Karli don't get the justice they deserve. Or the opportunities they deserve. I'm not willing to turn myself in until I get justice for my best friend."

"You're amazing," he breathed.

The fight she'd been holding on to slipped away while she let his compliment wrap around her. Jessica wasn't doing anything truly great. She was covering her own ass. But she honestly believed Karli's killer would never be caught if Jessica went to the police. They'd already made up their minds. It was up to Jessica to change them.

"I don't think I'm going to sleep again until I know you're okay. Will you stay here?"

"I haven't really thought about it."

"Stay. Dex and his team will be able to watch you. And you'll be safe here."

"I don't know if I can get answers here."

"Your safety is important, too." Braden rolled onto his back.

"I know, but the only way this ends is if I find out what's going on. I have to find that caller."

"Maybe I can get access to the call."

"Don't get yourself in trouble."

Braden chewed his cheek and nodded absently. "If Marcus was in charge, it would be a different story."

"But he's not. We can't do anything about it."

Braden looked over at her. "I don't know how you're so calm about all of this."

"I'm not calm. I'm trying to be rational and reasonable."

"And I just want this over so I can take you on another date."

"Is that all you want?" Jessica asked, laughing with him.

"Yep. I'm a simple guy. Food, work, and good company."

"I guess I haven't been very good company the last few days."

Braden rolled over on top of her and kissed her neck. "You've been the best company ever. But leaving here is going to be harder than you know."

Jessica spread her thighs and made room for him in between. He was thick and hard between them. Their gazes caught, and he shifted, his erection rubbing against her clit.

"Braden," she whispered. She didn't know when she'd see him again, or if, and letting him go without one last time was too painful to imagine.

He rolled over, grabbing the box of condoms they left on the nightstand. He put one on and was back between her thighs in less than a minute.

Braden didn't hesitate before he slid into Jessica. Her body tensed at the intrusion, but she relaxed and let him in, moaning when he slipped in all the way.

"God, you feel so good."

"You do, too."

Braden retreated, then pressed back inside, taking his time with slow, languid strokes. Each one left Jessica craving more.

It felt like they had time, like the first night when there was no rush. She closed her eyes and pretended they were back at his house, his dark wood bed beneath her and the bathroom across the hall. She wrapped her thighs around him and took him in deeper, delighting in the groan he let out.

Braden's thrusts increased in pace and depth, his control slipping ever so slightly. Jessica loved it when he lost all of his control and slammed into her hard. She prided herself on being able to do that to him. To make him unable to think and hold back.

He grunted above her. She looked up at him, focusing on Braden and only Braden. There was nothing and no one outside of the two of them and the moment they were in. She was going to enjoy it.

"Jessica," he grunted.

She got it. He was close, and he wanted her with him. "Touch me."

His eyes widened for half a second before they sank to half-mast and darkened. He wanted her to touch herself, but she was going to have plenty of time to make herself come when he left. Until then, she wanted him to do it.

He repositioned himself onto his knees without losing his momentum. The move lifted her hips off the bed and spread her even wider. His gaze traveled down her body to where he entered her, and he licked his lips.

"You're so beautiful."

He licked his thumb and, without taking his eyes from her, lowered his thumb to her clit. The first touch lifted her hips, her body seeking what he offered.

He dipped his thumb lower, stealing some of the moisture between them, then brought it back to her clit. The slippery flesh responded instantly, skyrocketing her orgasm to the heavens. It wasn't long before Jessica was begging Braden to let her come, and Braden was losing that last bit of control he held onto, slamming into her and rasping his thumb over her clit until neither of them had anything left to hold on to.

They tumbled together, bodies shaking and squeezing and releasing. Jessica heard Braden shout over her own screams of elation. He collapsed on top of her, his thumb still against her clit and his erection buried deep inside her.

She just laid there and held on, wishing the moment would last forever.

Braden started to slip from her body and pushed himself up. The friction of his movement sent an aftershock through Jessica that made Braden's lips turn up in a cocky grin.

"Oh, shut up," she said without any heat.

"You're stunning when you come."

"So are you," she confessed.

He winked at her, then disappeared into the attached bathroom. When he came back, Jessica hadn't moved.

"Are you going to lie here all day?" Braden asked.

"I wish," she said. Her unintentionally wistful tone had his smile faltering. She didn't mean to kill the mood, but they both knew the sex was goodbye.

Braden reached for her, pulling her up off the bed and into his arms. He slid one hand low on her hip and the other up to her neck, surrounding her with his presence.

Jessica tried not to cry. She wasn't an overly emotional person, but she was definitely struggling with that at the moment. Had been for two weeks.

They stood there for a few minutes, then went to the

kitchen for breakfast. They cooked in silence, both lost in their thoughts about the day.

The morning went far too quickly and before she knew it, they were having lunch. They didn't talk about Karli or Raina or anything really. They just existed together for their final few hours.

After lunch, Braden packed his truck.

"I have to be at work at six," he explained.

"I understand," Jessica said.

"I don't want to go."

"You don't have a choice. Do you have everything?"

"I think so. If not, I'll get it when I come back. I'm on shift for forty-eight hours, then I'll be back."

"Braden—"

"No. Don't tell me not to come back. I'm coming back. You have to promise me you'll be here."

Jessica smiled and stepped closer to him. "I was just going to say thank you."

He let out a rough exhale. He pulled her in close and kissed the side of her head. "I fucking hate this."

"Me, too."

They stood in each other's arms for a long few minutes.

"Promise me you won't leave. That you won't go anywhere else or do anything that could risk your life."

"I need to find out who killed Karli. If that requires me to leave—"

"Jessica, please. You need to stay here. I'll be back Monday night. Stay until then."

His voice was rough and harsh. He left no room for her to argue, even though she wanted to. She didn't want to go on the run again, and she definitely didn't want to be unsafe and homeless, but she bristled at his insistence.

"I don't like being told what to do."

He nodded. "I get that. And I would never. But this is about your safety. I won't be able to do anything if you leave here and something happens. I won't know where you are. I won't—"

"Okay. Okay. I'll stay."

He sighed a heavy sigh of relief. He closed his eyes and hugged her tight to him. "I need to know you're safe. Otherwise I won't be able to do my job. Thank you."

She nodded, but something inside was picking away at her trust. Something she couldn't quite put a finger on.

Braden hauled her in for another kiss that left her hanging on the edge of asking him to take her with him. She wasn't ready to be alone again, but she wasn't ready to go back.

"I'll be back in two days. I promise."

Jessica nodded. He got into the truck. She hit the button on the wall for the garage door to lift, and he started his truck. She forced a smile as he backed out, then pushed the button to close the garage again.

And he was gone.

Jessica stared at the closed door until the light inside the garage went out. She closed the door and locked it, then went to the couch.

It smelled like Braden.

Her throat swelled with the emotional she held back all day. After feeling like anything was possible with him by her side, Jessica was back to feeling like nothing was going to work out. She hated the person who killed Karli, for both taking her best friend and for ruining Jessica's life.

Jessica had friends who were on her side, but she knew that wouldn't last. How could they trust her when everything was stacking up against her? She needed to find the person who called nine-one-one. She had to know who it was and talk to them. Face-to-face. If she could understand why the person lied about her leaving, maybe she could get some answers about who actually killed Karli. It was very possible the caller killed Karli, but if they didn't, they had to know who did.

Jessica pushed aside the emotion that wanted to rule her and shook herself. She had to be rational and clear-headed. Which meant she could not let Braden leaving get to her. He'd be back in two days. Which meant she had two days to figure out what was going on. Then...they...could...

"Shit," she breathed.

Braden was the only person who knew where Jessica was. He was a firefighter. He saw everything as black and white. He wanted her to go back with him, to turn herself in. And she refused.

That didn't mean he gave up.

Was it possible Braden left so he could call the cops? So he could be the hero who found the fugitive?

Jessica struggled to believe it, but her mind wouldn't let go of the idea. If she were Braden, she never would have turned the other person in. But Braden was different. He couldn't imagine a world where there was a messy middle. For Jessica, that was where she lived.

Jessica growled at herself and shoved aside the idea that Braden could do something like that to her. He would never. She was being paranoid, and she had better things to do. Like find a killer.

She logged in to Dex's computer system and watched the lobby video for the hundredth time. It didn't show her anything new. Not that she expected it to, but she was hopeful.

She went through everything she'd already been through. She knew there had to be a recording on the nine-one-one call, but Dex still hadn't been able to get a hold of it. It was more than a little frustrating to feel like the answer was right there but not be able to grab it.

Jessica fixed herself an afternoon snack and came back to her research with a clear head. It didn't help, and by dinner, she was getting mad all over again.

"Okay, the caller had to have seen me to be able to describe me and know I was there. But the call came in before I went into Karli's apartment. So it had to be someone I either saw on the street or inside the building. I don't remember anyone in the building besides the guy who held the door, so maybe there was someone on the street."

Jessica talked to herself as she researched options. She felt a little crazy, but after talking things out with Braden over the last few days, she needed to say things.

She went through the footage they had from the cameras on the street. There weren't many, and no one stood out to Jessica. No one watched her when she walked by or made a call right after she passed them.

"Could it have been a resident?" she breathed.

Her entire body tingled at the idea that a killer could be right there in the building, with no one knowing he killed their neighbor. But it made the most sense.

Jessica sighed in frustration. There were no cameras in the building. She had no way of knowing if anyone who lived there went to Karli's apartment.

With no answers and a need for contact, Jessica logged in to social media. She knew it was a risk, but with all the security stuff Dex's team had on the computers, she doubted anyone would ever know.

She scrolled through photos of friends, not liking

anything. She wanted to be as carefree as they all appeared. Living their lives instead of running for them.

She was about to logout when a message blinked in the corner. She clicked over to it. It was an audio file. She hit play.

And gasped.

It was a recording. Of the nine-one-one call.

"Nine-one-one. What is your emergency?"

"I just saw a woman running out of my neighbor's apartment. She was covered in blood."

"Where are you, sir?"

"I'm hiding in my apartment," he whispered. "She went in, then came out a few minutes later covered in blood. I think she killed my neighbor."

"What is your address?"

"Nine-thirty-seven Mist Avenue. Apartment Three-E"

"And which apartment did the woman come out of?"

"Three-B."

"Okay. Thank you, sir. I have officers on the way. They will have to speak to you about what you saw."

"No. I don't want her to find out I'm the one who called. She might kill me, too. I know how those things work."

"The police will make sure your name is not released. They'll keep you safe."

"But when if she comes back?"

"Would you like me to stay on the line with you until the officers arrive?"

"No, no. I think she's gone. I'm just scared. Please tell the officers to hurry."

"They are, sir. They'll be there very soon."

"Thank you. Truly. Thank you."

The call ended, and Jessica nearly collapsed with relief. She had the call. And the caller. She didn't know his name, but he was Karli's neighbor. And he had to be her killer.

Jessica wanted to call Braden and tell him the news, but that was too big of a risk. And waiting two days? She couldn't do that either.

Jessica went to the bedroom and packed up her things. She shoved what she could into the sling bag she'd been using. She tied up the trash and hoped someone would get rid of it eventually.

Leaving was scary. She didn't really know where she was, but she knew she had no choice. She had to get back to the city and confront the man who called nine-one-one. He was the only one with the answers she needed.

Jessica used the computer once more to get directions back to the city. It was a long walk, almost seventeen miles. It was tempting to wait until morning, but it was safer to walk through the night. When fewer people were out and there was a lower chance she'd be recognized. That long of a walk would take most of the night, but she had no choice. She had food, and she was more rested than she'd been in weeks. She could do it.

And in the morning, it would all be over.

Jessica considered leaving a note for Braden but decided not to. If things went as planned, neither of them would have to go back to the safe house again. They would be free.

She double checked that she had everything she brought with her. She threw her bag over her shoulder and went to the front door. It felt strange to just walk out, but no one except Braden knew where she was. She was safe.

Outside was quiet as evening began. The automatic lock on the door engaged once she pulled it closed. Jessica smiled at the freedom she felt. She would face the man who called nine-one-one, she would get the evidence she needed to clear her name, and she would find Braden. Everything was going to work out.

Jessica walked down the front steps and stopped. The sound was faint, but it was definitely moving closer to her. She didn't have long.

Sirens. Lots of them.

13

———————

Jessica took off toward the woods surrounding the house. She wasn't sure if she had time to get away from the police before they swarmed what was supposed to be a safe house, but she was going to try.

She wasn't a runner, so by the time she reached the trees, she was out of breath and her muscles were screaming for relief. If she was ever free again, she was going to need to use the Birds of a Feather collection she had at home for something instead of lounging.

Jessica didn't stop when she got to the trees. She did slow down, but stopping would mean jail, and she'd come this far. She wasn't giving up yet.

The sirens screeched past her, moving toward the house. She was hidden from their view, but if they explored at all, they'd find her in a few minutes. She had to go.

Jessica pushed ahead. Every few feet she glanced back at the house she thought was safe. The house Braden told her to stay at for two days. The house he left just a few hours earlier, after making her promise she wouldn't leave.

Lights flashed, the spinning reflecting off trees near her. Jessica kept moving, deeper into the woods. She kept the road in sight, but she didn't dare go closer to it. She had to keep going. Her plan was to walk along the side of the road, but if the cops knew where she was, she had to stay hidden. Which meant going slower, spending the night in the woods, and not giving up.

Every step took her farther from the house and closer to reality. Her chest ached. Her muscles burned. Her entire body and mind screamed at her. She ignored all of it and kept going. She was numb. Like when she walked out of Karli's apartment with her best friend's blood on her hands. If she stopped to let the pain in, she'd fall apart.

That wasn't an option.

Tears streaked down her face, but she ruthlessly wiped them away. It wasn't time to cry. Not when she was in the fight of her life. She could cry for the loss of the man she loved later. When she'd cleared her name and left the city for good. She no longer had any doubts about leaving Niagara Falls. She couldn't work for Taylor and face Braden after he turned her in to the police. She couldn't stay in the same state as him. She would leave. Go far away where no one knew who she was and she could start over.

Karli would have wanted her to be happy. Her best friend understood Jessica in a way few others ever did. They were kindred spirits, and Jessica decided she was going to live the rest of her life for Karli. No matter how long that life was.

The sirens and lights faded as Jessica kept walking. Her shoes were good, but she wasn't prepared for a walk through the woods and they were getting damp.

Jessica didn't know how long she'd been walking, but it

felt like hours. She needed to rest. She glanced back the way she came and saw nothing but trees and darkness. The woods were quiet except for the chirping of crickets. It was getting cold, and the only option Jessica had was to keep going, even though every part of her demanded a long rest in a warm bed.

She slid her bag off her back and dug out a granola bar. It was dry and not very good, especially after the food she enjoyed at the safe house, but it was better than nothing. She swallowed some water, then started walking again.

Her pace slowed the longer the night dragged on. She kept the map in her mind, hoping she was going the right way. She should have printed the map out, but she was too used to having a phone to reference.

Stars lit her path, silently urging her on. Jessica figured she couldn't have walked more than a few miles before she had to rest again. The seventeen mile walk would have been tough on her best day, but that was not even close to her best day. And once she got to the city, she had to navigate to Karli's building without being caught so she could confront the man who called nine-one-one.

Every so often, a car passed her on the road to her left. The glow of headlights always shocked her, forgetting she was close to civilization until it jumped up in front of her. Jessica walked, counting her steps and trying to stay motivated.

And in her mind, she spoke to Karli. To her best friend. The person who would have gone on the run with her if she were alive. The person who would have been out in front of the press demanding people listen and convincing them all Jessica was innocent.

It was hard to imagine her life without Karli in it. The

only comfort she'd found in the last two weeks was Braden, and now that was gone, too. She just wanted to disappear forever, but she owed it to Karli to get justice. To find the person who killed her.

Jessica found a fallen tree at one point and sat down. She didn't hear anything out of the ordinary in the woods, so she told herself she could rest for a minute. Just a minute. Then she'd start moving again.

Just a minute.

"STACEY?" Braden answered the phone.

"Can you come to my office? I need to speak to you." Her voice was formal, official. Worried.

"Um, yeah. Does Wray need to come? We're still on shift. Is everything okay?"

"Everything's fine. I just need to talk to you. Only you."

Braden nodded and told her he'd be there shortly. Stacey hadn't called Braden much since they met. She was like a sister to him in a lot of ways, but they both knew their connection was because of Wray. If anything ever happened to Wray, Braden would take care of Stacey and the boys, but he admitted to himself it was because she was Wray's wife.

Braden told the battalion chief he had to run a personal errand, which earned him a glare but got him released, and drove across town to Shelter in the Storm. He parked on the street and got out of his truck. He walked up the steps to the front door and waited for someone to let him in.

"Good morning," Francesca, the owner, said. "How are you today?"

"I'm good, Francesca. How are you? How's everything going here?"

"We're not full, so I take that as a good sign."

Braden nodded. He had a lot of respect for Francesca. She opened Shelter in the Storm to help women and children who were victims of abuse. Stacey worked for her as a counselor. Between the two of them, they helped their guests repair their broken lives and move on from the abuse they suffered. It was admirable as much as it was sickening that it was needed. Braden knew Francesca saying they weren't full meant they had room for new guests if people showed up, which was the good thing, even though she wished her services weren't necessary.

"Stacey is waiting for us."

Braden's brows jumped in surprise. He assumed it was a partly social call from Stacey, but if Francesca was involved, too, something happened.

Braden followed Francesca down the hallway to the office at the back of the house. He glanced around as he walked, noting there weren't any women wandering around. He didn't know what they did all day, but he understood the need for privacy and wondered if they were simply avoiding him.

Francesca opened the door to the office and stepped back for Braden to enter. He smiled at her, then walked into the small room. Stacey was sitting in a chair in the corner, holding a woman's hands. The woman was crying.

Braden glanced back at Francesca. She closed the door and took the seat behind the large desk piled high with papers. She addressed Stacey and the woman like Braden wasn't even there. "Can you tell us again what happened?"

The woman lifted her watery gaze to Braden's. The despair in her eyes gutted him. He didn't know what she was about to say, but he knew it was going to hurt like hell.

"My name is Raina. We have a mutual friend. Two hours

ago, someone tried to kidnap me," she said, her gaze locked on his. "When I left here, I started taking walks early in the morning. It's quiet and I like the fresh air before the sounds and smells of the city change everything. It was part of me reclaiming my strength and independence from my ex. I love the freedom it gave me. But today when I got back, a man was waiting for me. He knew my name."

Braden wasn't sure what any of this had to do with him, but he didn't interrupt as Raina spoke.

"He said I had to go with him. That everything was going to work out. That I belonged to Damon, and he was there to take me to him." Raina hiccuped and wiped her nose. She accepted a tissue from Stacey, then drew a breath and closed her eyes.

Braden didn't know much about Raina or her situation, but it didn't take a genius to figure out Damon was the ex Jessica had mentioned. Whoever the man was that Damon sent to kidnap Raina didn't sound very smart if he told her what he was doing, but Braden wasn't going to point that out.

"He tried to knock me out, but he wasn't very coordinated. He missed when he lunged at me."

"I'm sorry, but why are you telling me all of this?"

"Because I think he lived in Karli's building. I'm sure I'd seen him before. Getting mail or something. I don't know his name, or which unit he lived in, but he looked familiar to me."

"Okay?"

"What Raina is saying is if her ex sent someone to kidnap her, it's also likely he sent the same man to kill Karli. Especially if he lived in the same building." Francesca raised one brow at Braden.

Braden looked at her, then Stacey and Raina, and still couldn't figure out what they were trying to tell him. "I'm sorry, but I don't get it. Why are you telling me all of this instead of Marcus or Lieutenant Juarez?"

"Because the man who tried to take me said he was going to be killed if he 'let one more bitch get away in less than twenty-four hours.'"

"What?" Braden breathed.

"He had to be talking about Jessica, right?" Stacey asked.

The words took a minute to penetrate the fog Braden's head was clouded by. Jessica was at the safe house. She was supposed to be safe. He was supposed to go back the next day to see her. She couldn't be gone. Or caught. Or on the run again.

"Do you know where Jessica is?" Francesca asked.

Braden looked at her, debating on what he should say. She was married to Captain Patrick. If Marcus wanted to know anything, it would be pillow talk and easy to get it out of his wife. Braden couldn't expect her to keep something like that from him.

"Braden, we think she's in danger," Stacey said.

"She was safe. No one knew where we were."

"He knew," Raina said. "I don't know how, but he knew. He said she got away. He said she wasn't supposed to this time, and that his balls were on the line for it."

"If she was caught, the police would be celebrating. They would have held a dozen press conferences." Braden wanted to pace the room, but it was too small. He ran a hand over his face and tried to think. What would she do? Where would she go? Why would she leave?

"I agree, which is why we think she's out there somewhere. Did you have a plan?" Stacey asked.

Braden nodded, his mind forgetting who he was talking to. "I told her to stay there. Not to leave. That I'd be back tomorrow night. I made her promise."

"Which means she's going to think you turned her in," Raina finished for him. "Did you?"

"No," Braden growled at her.

Raina stood from her seat, her tear-stained cheeks set firm. "Jessica was nice to me. She was funny and friendly, and I know she didn't kill Karli. I never believed it. When Stacey found me, I was scared out of my mind. I wasn't home when Karli... I saw the police cars and couldn't go into the building. I didn't know what happened, but I knew I couldn't go in there. Stacey called me and told me what Jessica said, then she brought me here. I thought I was done with him. But he killed my friend to get to me, and he'll do it again. He won't hesitate to kill anyone who gets in his way. And I'm done backing down from men like him who think they get to make all the rules."

"I didn't turn Jessica in. I know she's innocent. I wanted her to turn herself in, but she refused. I was being selfish when I asked her. If I could go back and not ask, I would, but I can't. I want her safe. I want her with me. And I want her free. That's what she deserves."

"Okay, so all of this is good, but we need to figure out what we're going to do," Francesca said. "We need to find Jessica and get her help. We need to figure out who the man is that tried to kidnap Raina. And we need to find Damon. End all of this."

"Sounds easy," Stacey said.

Raina snorted. "Completely simple."

"Where do we start?" Braden asked.

"You start by going back to work," Stacey said.

"No, I need—"

"Braden, we all understand this isn't easy for you, but there's a target on you. The police are watching your every move. The only reason you were able to come here today is because nothing happens inside this building without Marcus knowing about it, and he knows what happened with Raina. But if you don't go back for your shift, it's going to raise some flags."

"What am I supposed to say? Or do?"

"Do your job. And say nothing. If anyone asks, tell them a friend was in need. If the police come at you, tell them your relationship with anyone who is staying or visiting Shelter in the Storm is confidential and they need a court order to have any information." Francesca was not someone Braden wanted to mess with.

"I really can't do anything? How are you going to help Jessica?"

The three of them looked at him and smiled. "We hide in plain sight," Francesca said. "Like always."

"WHAT DO you mean she got away?" Damon growled. He was almost out of patience with the idiot. The messes he was making were not acceptable.

"She got away. I don't know what to tell you. I tried to jump out, but she fought back. Your bitch is fucking crazy."

Damon didn't hesitate before slamming his fist into the other man's ribcage. He felt the satisfying crunch of a rib breaking beneath his fist. In his younger years, he was a boxer and the joy of breaking bones was what led Damon to work for the Company. He garnered a reputation for having no mercy, refusing to stop fighting until the end of a round, even when his opponent wasn't fighting back.

He missed those days.

Silver howled like the fucking pussy he was and leapt away from Damon. "Fucking hell," he gasped. He clutched his side like that would stop the pain. "I think you broke my rib."

"That's for calling her fucking crazy. You say one more goddamn word about her and I'm going to kill you."

"Sorry, man. I didn't realize you were so sensitive about her."

"Tell me what happened," Damon demanded.

Silver's breath wheezed out of him. He winced when he tried to inhale. The break was small enough that it wouldn't kill him, but enough that he'd think twice before acting like he had any fucking leeway in how he behaved.

"I was waiting outside, like you said. She did the same thing as yesterday, going for a walk early in the morning, so I waited for her. I knew she'd be back in fifteen minutes. She came around the corner, and I jumped out at her. The cr— crafty woman reacted quickly and kicked me in the balls. I told her—"

"You talked to her?" Damon barked.

"Yeah. I mean, I told her she had to come with me."

"Did you tell her why?"

Silver avoided Damon's gaze for a second and shrugged.

Fucking hell. One broken rib wasn't enough for the stupid fucker. He needed his head smashed in like Raina's bitch of a roommate.

"I was trying to get her to my car, man. I didn't think she was going to get away."

"What exactly did you tell her?" Damon's voice offered no room for misunderstanding just how angry he was.

Silver swallowed audibly. "I told her I was taking her to

you. That she needed to come with me. And that I couldn't let two women go in twenty-four hours."

"Are you seriously that fucking stupid?"

Silver didn't answer.

Damon pulled his gun from his waistband and pointed it at the dumb fuck who just ruined the entire thing. With his confession to Raina, it wouldn't be long before the police were on him. And the son-of-a-bitch proved he couldn't be trusted. He would spill his guts to the cops in a heartbeat if he got arrested. He had to go.

"Wh— What are you going to do with that?" Silver sputtered.

"I'm going to shoot you in the fucking head."

"Wh— Why?"

"Because you not only told Raina everything, or enough to figure out I was behind her friend being killed, but you let her fucking go. What do you think she's doing right now? Getting her fucking nails done? No! She's telling the police everything you told her. How long do you think it's going to take them to figure out who you are and come after you? And if you're going to sing to Raina, why would I ever trust that you won't tell every cop who questions you everything? Why—"

A knock on the door stopped Damon's tirade.

"What?" Damon barked.

The door swung open. Mick took in the scene without flinching, then focused on Damon. "The boss needs to see you. Now."

"Why?"

Mick shrugged. "Didn't say. But we have to go right now."

Damon glared hard at Silver. "You got a reprieve. For

now. Don't leave this fucking building. I'll deal with you when I get back."

Damon ignored Silver, and the wet mark on the front of his pants, and followed Mick out of the building to the waiting SUV. What fucking shit did he have to deal with now?

14

———

DAWN FINALLY ARRIVED. AGAIN. JESSICA WAS COLD AND TIRED. Her feet felt like she'd been sitting in a tub for days. She was hungry.

But above it all, she was heartbroken. Braden betrayed her. He told the police where she was. If she wasn't on her way out the door when they arrived, they would have caught her.

She hated it. It left an ache inside of her that would never go away. But she had a job to finish. She was going to get a confession out of the man who killed Karli, clear her name, and build a new life. Far away from Braden Wright.

The plan was to have everything done and settled the day before, but walking through the woods slowed Jessica down. She didn't get as far as she'd hoped, and when dawn came the morning before, she was still miles away from Niagara Falls. She spent the day blending in and doing her best not to draw any attention to herself. She finally made it to the city, but evening arrived and she hesitated.

Facing the person who killed her friend was harder than

Jessica thought. Every time she tried to think of what to say to him, she broke down.

But reality was closing in. Jessica was running out of options. The police would find her. They'd been on her heels for two weeks, showing up everywhere she went just moments after she left. If she was going to confront the person who called nine-one-one, the man Jessica believed killed Karli, time was running out. It had to happen now.

Jessica wanted to stop and get breakfast before her walk to Karli's building, but her cash was running out. The last two nights were her longest yet. She thought the first night on the streets was endless, but she was able to sit down and rest. Walking miles and miles and miles through the woods, knowing she was being stalked by the police, was terrifying. And after feeling safe for four days with Braden, living with his betrayal made it all that much harder.

It would all be over soon. When she had answers and the man who killed Karli was behind bars. And Jessica was able to leave Niagara Falls and never come back.

The edge of the city, where she spent the night, was quiet. The streets were narrow and only a handful of cars passed. Jessica kept her head down as she walked along the side of the road. It wouldn't be long before there were side-walks and people she could blend in with, but until then, it was best to avoid looking up.

The sun warmed her body as she kept going. She was so focused on keeping her head down that she didn't notice the car that pulled to the side of the road until she almost walked into it.

"Jessica," a voice hissed.

Instinct had her lifting her head at the sound of her name. She tried to fight it, but it was too late.

"Stacey?" Relief filled her veins. "What are you doing here?"

"Looking for you. Get in."

"I can't. You'll get in trouble, too."

"I want to help you. And the only way I can do that is if you get in. Now."

Jessica hesitated again, but her desire for help and to get off her feet overwhelmed her unease. She climbed into the front seat of Stacey's car and buckled her seatbelt as Stacey eased away from the side of the road like she had all the time in the world.

"How did you find me?"

"Marcus told Frannie the cops went to the safe house. Braden told me where it was. I've been looking for you since yesterday morning."

"Let me out," Jessica demanded. "Pull over. If you're working with Braden, I need to get out." She tried to tug the handle, but the doors were locked.

"Braden didn't send the police," Stacey said, continuing to drive. "I promise you."

"No one else knew where I was. If it wasn't Braden, then who was it?"

"I don't know, but Braden wouldn't lie to me about that. When I told him the police were there, he freaked out."

"He said Dex and English mentioned the safe house. Could one of them...?" Jessica trailed off before she finished the question. She couldn't imagine her boss's boyfriend turning her in. Or anyone else he worked with.

"No, I doubt it. They've been keeping an eye on you, but they wouldn't turn that over. I think they've been getting in some trouble because of it."

"That's the last thing I wanted. No one should have to

suffer because they know me. God, Stacey, you have little kids. They'll take your boys from you for helping me."

"They will not," Stacey said firmly. "Because I'm doing nothing wrong because you did nothing wrong. You adored Karli. She was your best friend in the world. I saw how you two were. There was a comfortable familiarity that doesn't happen unless you are close. I know her death is painful for you. And I know you are not the kind of person who would ever hurt someone else, but especially someone you loved so much."

Jessica drew a deep, ragged breath and nodded. "It hurts. A lot. Which is why I'm not turning myself in."

"I never asked you to. Do you know why Braden had to come to my house the morning after your first date?"

Jessica's cheek heated. "You knew about that?"

"That you were at his house when Wray called? Yeah. Do you know why Wray called?"

Jessica shook her head.

"I was arrested."

"What?"

"One of my clients was killed, and I was determined to prove her ex-husband killed her. I was following him, and he almost killed me a few times. I finally caught up to him and was going to call the cops, but he was dead. The cops found me in the same room as his body, holding the knife that was used to kill him."

"Oh my God."

"It looked like a suicide, but his daughter is convinced someone killed him. I think she's right. I'm not unhappy he's dead, but anyway... All of that is besides the point. If you're going to prove you didn't kill Karli, and avoid the police, you need help."

"And you're going to help me?"

Stacey dug into her purse and pulled out something small and black.

"What is this?" Jessica took it and opened it up. "A mask?"

Stacey nodded. "My boss, Frannie, she gave that one to me. Her story is hers to share, but she helped find a killer years ago wearing that mask. I was wearing it when I found Oscar. And I think you need it now."

"Is it magical?" Jessica asked with a laugh.

"I wish. When I wore it, I felt powerful. Like I wasn't alone. You're going to face whoever killed Karli. And when you do, you might be alone. I want you to know we'll be behind you, no matter what."

Jessica stared at the tiny scrap of fabric. It was black with a little sparkle. She couldn't imagine it would change much, but the idea of not being alone was nice. She didn't know Stacey well, but she appreciated the gesture more than Stacey would ever know.

"Thank you."

"You're welcome. Use it wisely, and bring down whoever did this. I wish there was more I could do for you."

"Did you ever find Raina?"

Stacey nodded. "She's safe. But her ex tried to have her kidnapped yesterday morning. By someone Raina thinks lived in Karli's building. She got away."

"What?"

"He knew where she was somehow, kind of like someone always seems to know where you are. The guy who tried to grab her was waiting for her. He told her he was supposed to take her to Damon. But she's strong. She fought him off and got away."

"Thank God she's okay. I would never forgive myself if she got hurt, or any of you, because of all of this."

"You are not responsible for all of this, Jessica. You are trying to make it right. Just like I was doing for Holly. Getting justice for a friend is never the wrong choice in my mind."

"Even if it hurts others?"

Stacey reached over and grabbed Jessica's hands. "If it hurts people who would hurt you, that's on them. They shouldn't have been involved. Holly's husband was evil. He killed her in broad daylight because he hated that she got away from him. He stole their daughter's childhood from her. He deserves to be dead for what he did. I wish I knew who killed him because I think Vera needs that closure, but the police are convinced it was suicide. But none of that means Oscar was innocent. He wasn't. Maybe he didn't deserve to die, but neither did Holly."

"Or Karli."

"Exactly. I had no intention of killing Oscar, and I didn't. I wanted him to sit in jail for the rest of his life and think about what he did to Holly. Think about how it hurt his daughter. I wish he could have done that, but I'm guessing he knew things he wasn't supposed to know and someone took care of him."

A chill raced down Jessica's spine. "That's what I want for Karli's killer. I hope I get the chance to deliver justice to him."

"Him? Do you think you know who it is?"

Jessica nodded hesitantly.

"But you don't want to tell me." It wasn't a question.

"I can't, Stacey. I need to know for sure. Before I call the police. I need to know why."

"I understand. I want you to know the police are moving slowly on Raina's kidnapping case. They haven't arrested anyone and have no suspects yet. They can't have her look through photos of everyone in the building. Not without more information about who the man was."

"Even if she thinks he lived there?" Jessica asked. The pieces were clicking into place, and it was sounding like exactly what she feared. Raina's ex was behind Karli's death, and he wasn't done. He wouldn't be done until he had Raina back. Jessica was not going to let that happen.

"They have to protect the innocent people who live there. We know Raina isn't lying, but someone could say they were attacked so they could find out where someone lives. Raina isn't going to give up trying to find the man, or fighting back against Damon."

"I'm glad she's not alone."

"No, she's not. And neither are you. Promise me one thing," Stacey said, pulling into a parking space on the side of the road and putting the car in park.

"What?"

"Promise me you'll be safe. And that you'll call if you need anything."

Jessica nodded. "I promise."

Jessica unbuckled her seatbelt and leaned across the car to hug Stacey. They held each other tight for a few minutes, then Jessica released her friend. She got out of the car, but Stacey called out once more.

"I forgot. I packed you food. It's in bags so you don't have big things to carry. A breakfast sandwich and coffee for right now, and some healthy snack options for later. Just in case."

Jessica's eyes welled with tears. She reached in and took the offered bags and paper cup. "Thank you."

"I'll see you soon."

"Hopefully not on the news."

Stacey breathed a laugh. "I agree. Take care, Jessica."

Jessica nodded and closed the door. She stepped back

from the curb and watched as Stacey pulled away. When she turned the corner, Jessica looked around to see where she was.

And found herself three blocks from Karli's apartment. And the killer's.

DAMON STOMPED around his office and seethed. That little weasel fucked him. He was not going to get away with it. Damon was going to enjoy killing him.

As soon as he found the fucker.

A knock on his door had him growling. "What?"

The door opened, and Mick stepped in.

"Anything?"

Mick shook his head. "Nothing. We have no idea where he is."

"Fuck!" Damon shouted. He swiped everything off of his desk, feeling slightly better when it shattered on the floor. He faced his desk and put his hands on the edge, staring at the wall. Where could Silver have gone? The son-of-a-bitch wasn't smarter than Damon, so why the fuck couldn't Damon figure out where he was?

His people had searched the man's apartment, his favorite hangouts, and his work. No one had seen or heard from him. If they did too much digging, they could tip off the wrong person and bring more attention to the Company. Something Damon already had his ass handed to him about.

Well, if Silver had done his fucking job, Damon wouldn't have forgotten about the shipment. It was on Silver that the guns they were supposed to have delivered didn't get delivered. If Silver hadn't stolen something from Raina and had kept an eye on Jessica like he was supposed to, Damon would have been able to focus on his job instead of trying to clean up after the worthless fucker who couldn't do anything right.

"What do you want to do, Boss?" Mick asked.

Damon hung his head and snarled. He didn't know. He needed to find Silver and put an end to the man who caused so much trouble. Confessing who Silver was and why he was working for Damon was hard to admit to his boss. The truth did not go over well. Damon knew who really ran the Company, but he couldn't officially take over, yet. He would, though. One day. When he had Raina by his side and couldn't be stopped.

"I want to find that slippery fucker and make him regret sneaking out of here after I left last night. How is it possible we don't have him on any cameras?"

Mick shrugged. "Don't know, sir. Hard to imagine he had the brains to figure out how to turn them off, or could avoid them."

"He's dumber than a brick wall. And thinking he could get away from me is proof. We need to find him."

"What about the shipment? The boss said—"

"I know what the boss said," Damon snapped. His ass was going to be on the chopping block if the deal fell through a second time. Damon was the one responsible because he was the one who could handle it. Failure wasn't an option. Especially not a second time.

"So, what are we going to do? The shipment is getting delivered in an hour."

Damon growled. He hadn't slept, hadn't eaten, and hadn't fucked in hours. He was tired, hungry, and horny, and he couldn't fix any of them. "Did the boss send over anything for me?"

Mick's brows jumped with shock before he quickly schooled them. "Um, no, sir."

More evidence Damon was on the shitlist. He was a fan of the guns they brought into the area and always took a few for himself. The drugs he only used on rare occasions these days. The women were usually strung out and far too skinny for Damon. He liked a woman who could handle a good, hard fucking, not one who could barely stand long enough to take it. The boss had started giving him first go at some of the new merchandise. Before the women were hooked on whatever drugs they had pumped into their systems. They were eager to please and happy to fuck.

But that week's gift hadn't arrived. Which meant Damon was no longer a favorite. He had to prove himself again, or he'd lose his chance to take over when the boss inevitably fucked it all up and brought the Company down.

Damon growled and pushed away from his desk. "Get someone to clean this shit up. I need food. Then we have a deal to save and a weasel to skin."

Mick nodded and followed Damon out of the office. Damon went outside and got into the waiting SUV, trusting his new driver had already been told where they were going. It was not the day for Damon to be answering questions and leading someone around by the nose.

They went through a drive-thru and got food for both of them. Damon sat in the back and angrily ate his breakfast, hating every bite. He was still tired and horny, but those things had to wait. He had a deal to seal and a boss to please. He lost sight of things once, and he couldn't let the boss think he wasn't back on track.

His life depended on it.

15

BRADEN WAS READY FOR HIS SHIFT TO BE OVER. HE SPENT THE last twenty-four hours ready to claw at his skin. He reached out to Dex, but Dex didn't know where Jessica was. No one knew anything. No one could do anything. Including Braden.

"What's wrong with you?" Wray asked early in the morning after they got back from a call.

It had been a full day since Braden spoke to Stacey. Since he found out Jessica was on her own again. He hadn't been able to voice his fear that he might never see her again.

"Okay. How about where did you go yesterday morning? Because you've been on edge since then," Wray said.

"Stacey called me."

Wray's brows shot up. "My Stacey?"

Braden nodded.

Wray's eyes narrowed. "What's going on?"

Braden looked around the weight room and shook his head. He jerked it toward the door and led the way to the bunks. He checked to make sure no one was sleeping or hanging around, then dropped onto one of the beds.

Wray sat opposite him and waited.

Braden finally looked up at his friend. "I was with Jessica. At a safe house. Dex told me where it was, and I found Jessica after our last shift and took her there. I only came back for this shift because PD was going to arrest me if I didn't show up, and I'd lose my job."

"Fucking hell. Is Jessica okay? Where is she?"

"That's why Stacey called me. I left her at the safe house, but a few hours later, the cops showed up there."

"You turned her in?"

"No!" Braden glared at his friend. "I wouldn't."

"You think the world is black and white. That people are good or bad. When she ran, you thought she was guilty because innocent people don't run. That's changed now?"

"She's innocent. It was instinct. She ran because she was scared. She didn't kill her friend. That's not who she is."

"I'm glad you finally realize that."

Braden nodded. "It took me a little while, but I got there."

"Okay, but she hasn't turned herself in. Do you think that means she's guilty?"

Braden shook his head. "I asked her to. I don't know what the right thing is, though. She wants to figure out who killed Karli, and why, and I get that. But I did not tell the police where she was. I have no idea who did. No one knew we were there except Dex and his team, and they're the ones who told us to go there. They're in danger of losing their contracts because they aren't willing to cooperate with the police on this."

"That's not good, but it sure is admirable."

"Yeah," Braden said absently.

"You don't agree?"

Braden shook his head. His mind was jumbled. He

agreed with Dex's choice to keep Jessica safe. He knew it was the right thing to do. He couldn't stand the idea of her going to jail. But he also believed in the system. In the police doing what was right. In justice being in the hands of the courts and not in the hands of an individual.

But the two couldn't work together. The gray zone was getting bigger.

"Jessica is innocent. I have no doubt about that. But I know she's right that the police aren't even considering someone else could be to blame. They're all in on her being the killer. So if she's caught, it's over."

"I agree." Wray drew a breath and stood. He paced to the other side of the bunk room and back. "Are you going to tell me what any of this has to do with Stacey?"

"She's the one who told me the safe house was exposed. Marcus told Francesca, and she told Stacey. I met with them and Raina at Shelter in the Storm. Someone tried to kidnap Raina early yesterday morning."

"Whoa. That's... Is she okay? Why didn't Stacey tell me any of this?"

Braden nodded. "You've been here. The only reason she told me is because of Jessica. The person who tried to kidnap Raina said he was there under orders of her ex. When Karli was killed, Jessica told Stacey to get in touch with Raina in case the person who killed Karli was really after Raina. Raina thinks the guy lived in Karli's building."

Wray blew out a breath of exhaustion. "Shit. This is complicated."

"Yeah. And Jessica is missing, out there somewhere. And I'm stuck here with no way of finding her or helping her."

"Do you think she went after him?"

"No. If this guy is the one behind it, Jessica won't know that. I have no idea where she would have gone, where she would be hiding. But wherever she is, she thinks I called the cops on her."

"Probably," Wray said with a snicker.

"It's not fucking funny. How would you feel if Stacey thought that?"

"Well, Stacey's my wife and my everything. I'm hoping she would know I didn't do that. Have you told Jessica you're in love with her?"

"I'm not," Braden protested.

Wray lifted one brow. "Really?"

"Yeah, I..."

Wray chuckled. "Yep. That's what I thought."

"I—"

The alarm went off, stopping Braden's thoughts. It was go time. And he couldn't let anything else get in his way. He had to stay focused or people could die. He could evaluate his feelings for Jessica later.

JESSICA TIED her hair back and put a hat on her head to hide the rest of her dark hair. If she had makeup, she would have tried to disguise herself, but she was out of luck. The only thing she could do was pull her hood low over her face and try to avoid the cameras in the lobby when she managed to get inside.

Walking up to Karli's building again made her entire body shake. It was the last place she wanted to be, a realization she didn't have until she tried to open the door and found herself unable to do it. A young mom struggled to get her stroller and toddler out of the building, and Jessica stepped up to help. She held the door for them and smiled at the frazzled and grateful woman before letting the door fall closed.

Jessica walked away from the building and shook her hands to get rid of the uneasy feeling. She had to go inside. To climb the stairs to Karli's floor and confront the man who killed her.

Jessica dug into her bag again, trying to find something that would help hide her identity. Her fingers brushed the mask Stacey gave her. In the few minutes since they parted ways, Jessica had forgotten about it. Her fear and the memories from the last time she walked into the building were too much, and the mask was buried.

It was a simple mask, plain and worn. She couldn't imagine it would actually do anything for her. She lifted it to her face and rolled her eyes. It was silly. Wear a mask. She shook her head and stuffed it back into her bag.

She walked to the door again. She passed by when no one was there to let her in. Her entire body trembled once more. Karli's skull. The blood. The sickening softness of her head.

Jessica hurried away, crossing the alley and finding a trash can to empty her stomach. People stepped away from her in disgust. She tried to breathe, but her stomach flipped again. She stuck her head in the trashcan once more, heaving until nothing came up.

Jessica straightened and wiped her mouth on the back of her hand. She backed away from the trashcan and dug her water bottle out of her backpack. She swished the water in her mouth, trying in vain to get rid of the horrible taste. She spit the water into the trashcan and walked down the street away from the building.

She couldn't do it. She couldn't walk into there and pretend like it was normal. Like she belonged. Her best friend was dead. And facing the man who called nine-one-one and probably killed Karli was more than she could handle. She had to figure out something else.

Jessica walked until she came to a park a few blocks away. She slowed her pace. The park was quiet, peaceful. There was a runner on the other side. Two parents chatted and pushed kids on swings. An older couple strolled ahead of her, holding hands.

The fall flowers were wilting and dying. The leaves on the trees were dull reds, oranges, and yellows. Leaves sprinkled the ground. The cold weather was not far off.

Fall was Karli's favorite time of year. She loved football and leaves changing and chilly nights around a fire pit. Her thirty-fourth birthday would have been in a few weeks. Instead, she was gone.

And the person who killed her was free.

Jessica sat on a bench and closed her eyes. She brought back her last memory of Karli, when she was alive. They were talking about life and love and what they were hoping to find one day. Raina was talking about her ex, and Karli looked at her with all the sympathy of a friend who wanted to protect and love her.

At one point, Karli looked at both of them and made them promise they would help her bury the body if she ever met Damon. Raina laughed, but Jessica agreed without hesitation. No one should ever go through what Raina went through. Jessica agreed with Karli that the man didn't deserve to be on the topside of the dirt.

The conversation was mostly in jest, but it was the one and only time Jessica wished someone was dead. Raina was so beautiful, inside and out, and knowing what Damon put her through, the horrors he inflicted on her, made Jessica sick.

Just like seeing Karli's skull smashed in made her sick.

Jessica had no proof Raina's ex had anything to do with Karli's death, but if he had someone try to kidnap Raina, Jessica doubted he wasn't involved. Damon was evil and heartless, from what Raina said, and killing Karli and framing Jessica was an easy way to leave Raina vulnerable. If Jessica was ever going to prove it, she had to walk into that building and face the man who told the police she killed Karli.

Jessica reached for the mask again. She drew a breath and shook her head at herself, then put it on.

And knew she could do it.

For Karli. And Raina. And Stacey's friend Holly. And all the other women who never got the justice they deserved.

Jessica pushed off the bench and stalked back to Karli's building. She ignored the snickers and eye rolls she got from people passing by and kept walking like she was on a mission.

When she got to the building, her stomach fluttered but didn't revolt. A man was walking out in a hurry and let the door dangle from his fingers to let her in. She thanked him and ducked her head as she rushed inside and to the stairs.

The stairway was blissfully empty as Jessica moved up from the ground floor. She kept her head down, but she didn't pass another person. When she got to Karli's floor, Jessica turned down the hall and drew a deep breath for strength.

Karli was with her. Protecting her. Helping her. She was going to find the truth. Now.

Jessica wasn't sure how she was going to get into the apartment to see the man from the call. She walked down the hallway toward his door, trying to come up with a story that would work. Something that would get him to let her inside.

She realized there wasn't anything that would make him talk to her and admit the truth. If he did kill Karli, he wasn't going to just tell her. Not unless he was going to kill her, too. And Jessica really didn't want that to happen.

She lifted her hand to knock on the door and paused. What if she just walked into his apartment? No. She shook her head. She wasn't a criminal, and she had no intention of becoming one.

Jessica knocked on the door. She felt silly standing there in her mask and knocking, but when she asked the man if he killed her friend, it wouldn't matter what she was wearing.

No one answered the door after a few seconds, so Jessica knocked again. Harder. Some of the apartments were big, and if someone was in another room, they might not have heard her knocking.

This time, when she knocked, the door popped open.

The same thing happened when she went to Karli's.

Jessica's stomach flipped. If she hadn't already emptied it, she might be searching for a trashcan.

"Hello?" Jessica called out. She pushed the door open wider and stepped inside. She closed her eyes and tried to shove the memories of Karli from her mind.

The apartment was far from clean. Dishes filled the sink in the kitchen to the left. The couch was stained and dirty. Pizza boxes covered a coffee table in the middle of the living room. A desk drawer was pulled free of the desk near the window and dumped onto the ground.

A chill raced up Jessica's spine.

"Is anyone here?" she called out.

She stepped inside, lifting her feet to avoid tripping on

the half dozen pairs of shoes at the door. The bedroom door was open to the right, an unmade bed the only thing visible from the entryway.

"Hello?" Jessica tried again. "Your door was open."

Jessica walked a few more feet, trying to talk herself into checking the bedroom. If someone was there, he could be hiding. Or he could be hurt. She didn't want to go to be accused of a second murder she didn't commit, but she struggled to walk away when someone could be hurt.

"Is anyone here?"

Jessica took another step toward the bedroom when she heard the floor creak.

"Hello? I don't want to scare you. Are you okay? I just wanted to ask you a few questions."

She moved toward the creak, hoping whoever was in the bedroom was friendly. She had her doubts given where she was and why, but she needed answers, and that desire pushed her forward.

"Hello?" Jessica said softer, slowly pushing the bedroom door open.

Before she could get into the room, the door swung back at her. A growl shocked her half a second before the door slammed into her, knocking her against the frame. She crumpled to the floor.

"You're not going to kill me!" a man shouted.

Jessica tried to regain her balance and stand, but he kicked her in the stomach.

"Did he really think you would be able to surprise me?"

He swung at Jessica, but she managed to dodge the hit. He howled when he connected with the doorframe.

"You bitch. What the..." He stopped and laughed. "You're the friend. Well, well. It looks like I need to call the police. Let them know there's a killer in my apartment."

"There always has been a killer in your apartment," Jessica forced out. "You killed Karli, not me. So, yeah, call and confess. They'll be happy to hear the truth."

The man turned back to her and smiled with all his teeth. Yellow, crooked teeth surrounded by cracked lips. His skin was sunken around his eyes, an unhealthy yellowish color. He was skinny and greasy and looked like he'd been on the business end of far too many needles. If Jessica ran into him in public, she'd think he was homeless and pity him. But that smile... That smile was pure evil. That smile was one of a man who knew exactly how dangerous he was, and exactly how to yield his power.

"What makes you say that, Jessica German?"

"Because you called nine-one-one. You reported me running from the building before I was even in her apartment. How would you know she was dead if you didn't kill her?"

"That's not what the police think. The police saw the videos I provided. The ones that show you were in the building long before I made that call."

"That's not true. I didn't kill her. She was my friend."

He pouted at her. "I know. Although all the stories on the news make you sound truly horrific. How could anyone ever think you're innocent? You are an evil woman, Ms. German."

"I am not! You're evil. And everyone is going to know what you did to Karli. You're going to pay for it."

He threw his head back and laughed. His scrawny throat stretched with the move, his thin skin loose and floppy. He howled with laughter like she told him the best joke ever.

And Jessica knew going to his apartment alone was quite possibly the biggest mistake of her life. And the last.

16

BREATH HEAVED FROM JESSICA, PAINFUL AND RAGGED. SHE stared up at the man above her, wondering how a person became so evil. That was exactly what he was. Evil.

"What are you doing in my apartment, Jessica German?" he asked, his voice slithering up her spine. He moved around her, keeping his dark eyes locked on her beneath him on the floor.

"I came to ask why you called the police on me. Why you told them I killed my friend."

The man rubbed his chin and smiled. There was a glint in his eyes, like he was remembering the whole thing. Like he enjoyed taking a life. Taking Karli's life.

Jessica had never known that kind of evil before. She'd never witnessed it. It chilled her to her very core. It made her wonder if there was a light at the end of the tunnel. It drowned out the good she was used to feeling in the world.

"Have you ever taken a life?" the man asked.

Jessica swallowed roughly. She was sure it was a rhetorical question. Most people didn't assume others were murderers. She stared up at the man, waiting for him to continue.

"Have you?" he growled, gnashing his teeth at her.

"No. Of course not," she rushed to say. She jumped back to get away from him, her back hitting the doorframe, and wished she could crawl inside the walls and disappear. Or that she could turn back time and never walk into the building or his apartment.

He snickered like she was a foolish child and he was wise. "Of course not. Such innocence."

He leaned down and cupped her jaw. She jerked away from him, but he held firm, turning her head so she had no choice but to meet his angry, twisted gaze.

"I can still remember the first time I took a life. It wasn't on purpose then, but it was the first time I felt good. The first time I knew what I was meant to do with my life."

"You think you were meant to kill people?" she squeaked. Fear lifted inside of her and filled her veins. She was never going to see the light of day again. Never see her friends and family. Never see Braden.

Never tell Braden she loved him.

Jessica worked hard to avoid regrets. She lived her life in a way that left no room for them. She loved her job and her family, even though she didn't see them often, and she spent time with friends who mattered. She did everything she could to make sure the people she was close to knew she cared about them. Except Braden.

She'd been afraid to tell him how she felt. After only one date, he would have thought she was crazy. Even after spending days together in the safe house, it felt far too soon. But now, she just wished she could see him one more time. That she could tell him how amazing he was and to always fight for what was right. He was one of the good ones. The kind of man she'd always wanted to have in her life. The kind of man she hoped to find one day. The kind she waited for.

And he was never going to know how amazing she thought he was.

The man in front of her caught her attention again. He shrugged, shifting her chin with the slight movement. A vacant look filled his gaze, one that was somehow more chilling than the evil look he gave her when he talked about killing Karli.

"I was driving down a dark road. It was late. I was young, too young to be driving legally, but my dad was a drunk and my mom was a whore and most of the time they neither cared nor knew what I was doing or where I was. So, I took the truck out to go see this girl I liked. I was the only person our age who knew how to drive. The girl was afraid to go for a drive with me, but she let me into her room. After we fucked, I was going back home in the truck. The road had a sharp turn, a blind curve, and on the other side, there was a woman walking on the side of the road. I tried to avoid her, but by the time I saw her, I hit her."

Jessica's breath stuttered to a stop. She couldn't fathom it. He was far too nonchalant about hitting a woman with his vehicle. Like it didn't bother him at all.

"I got out, and she was lying there. She moaned. Her skirt had lifted up, and she had these curvy legs and blue lace panties on. Her knee was bent at an awkward angle. It turned me on so much that I couldn't stop myself from walking closer to her. She was beautiful. The blood running down her cheek, the wild look in her eyes, the moaning that reminded me of the way the girl I liked moaned when I fucked her."

Jessica closed her eyes. She couldn't look at him. She knew what was coming next.

He shook her chin, forcing her eyes to open. He was smiling again. "I had an extra condom in my pocket, so I put it on. I didn't want to leave any trace. When I entered her, she cried out, but I saw the look in her eyes. She was just as excited as I was."

Tears rolled down Jessica's cheeks. She couldn't imagine the pain the woman had been in, and then to be raped when she couldn't fight him off. He was a monster.

"You're sick," Jessica said.

He shook his head. "No. I just take what I'm owed."

"You weren't owed anything. You hit that woman, then raped her."

"Yeah, well, she never told anyone." He stood up and laughed. "She died on the side of the road. No one ever knew I was there. My dad went to jail for it. Since they found her blood on his truck."

"Oh, my God," Jessica breathed.

"She got justice. Someone went to jail for her murder. And I got a new truck out of the deal. One with good memories. After that, I knew how good it felt to take a life. To take anything I wanted."

Jessica let out a sob. He was sick. Twisted and disturbed. She just thought he was a liar, but he was so much worse than she ever imagined.

He stared above her head. She tried to commit everything about him to memory, in case she ever had a chance to tell someone who he was. From his greasy hair to his gray eyes to his hollow cheekbones and frail figure. If she had to guess, he was a drug addict. What was surprising was he could afford to live in Karli's building. She'd never seen anyone else who looked like him, and the apartments weren't cheap. Jessica wondered how he paid his rent. And what other things he was involved in.

"After her, it was easy. Mostly people no one missed. A good way to perfect my skills. Your friend was a new challenge. One I was rewarded for with a bounty on my head."

"Who put a bounty on your head?" Jessica asked, hoping she could keep him talking until someone figured something out. Who and what, she wasn't sure, but she had to hold on to whatever hope was out there.

"You don't need to know about that. I thought that's why you were here. They already checked for me, though. No coming back here without arising suspicion. They're not the kind of people who blend in. That's why I was the one who got to kill your friend."

"Why? What did she ever do to you?"

"Nothing," he admitted. "I didn't even know her. Said hi once, I think, but it wasn't personal for me. I just liked to kill people. And I guess I was in the right place at the right time."

"She didn't deserve to die."

Jessica wanted to record his confession. To make sure the police knew everything. But when she showed up at his apartment and the door swung open, she forgot all about it. Now, after being trapped inside with the psycho, she couldn't get the recording device she snagged from the safe house out without him noticing. He hadn't taken his eyes off her since he knocked her to the floor.

"We're all going to die, eventually. There is no deserving or not, it's just fact."

"She didn't deserve to be murdered."

He shrugged. "I think we all deserve to be murdered. It's the purest form of admiration. She wasn't alone when she died. She was able to just drop and fall asleep."

Jessica's eyes filled with tears. Her heart pounded hard. She wanted to attack him, make him regret what he did, but there was no way that would happen. Not with a man like him. Not when he was cold and absent of any feeling.

"Would you like to hear how I killed her?"

Jessica cried harder and shook her head. She wanted to know everything because she wanted to change it for her friend, but there was no fixing it. There was no bringing Karli back, and knowing the truth about the man who smashed in the back of her skull wouldn't soothe anything inside Jessica.

"Oh, I don't believe that. I think you want to know. You want to hear about how I snuck down to her apartment after I saw her come home. I waited almost thirty minutes. Until she was relaxed and comfortable inside. Because I'm considerate like that."

"Please," Jessica begged. "Don't."

"Oh, see, she didn't beg. Let me tell it. She wasn't very smart. Her door was already unlocked when I went in. I was ready to use my key, but she left it open. I walked inside, and she was right there. In front of me like a gift. A beautiful gift like the woman the first night."

"No," Jessica breathed.

"She didn't see me, which gave me a minute to admire her curly hair and the curve of her body. She was a beautiful woman. I would have enjoyed spending time with her if I'd had more of it, but I knew I had to be quick. There was a brick on the table by the door. It was a strange trinket for a woman to have, but it came in handy for me. I lifted it, testing the weight of it, and swung. It came down hard on the back of her head, the crack making the most beautiful sound."

"No," Jessica cried. She rocked back and forth, trying to

block out his voice. She didn't want to know. She didn't want the image in her mind for the rest of her life, even if that was a painfully short time.

"She dropped fast. Faster than anyone else I've ever killed. That block was solid and strong. I thought I'd have to hit her again, but unfortunately, I didn't. She didn't even twitch when she hit the floor. Her beautiful hair was soaked, her brain leaking into it. It was gorgeous." He inhaled, closing his eyes like he was remembering a field of flowers and a peaceful afternoon instead of Karli's dead body.

"She didn't deserve that."

"Oh, but she did. She crossed the wrong person, apparently. I was only delivering his message."

"What was the message? Because it sounds like she never got it."

He snorted, laughing at her and shaking his head. "She got the message. Trust me."

Jessica stared at him through her tears. Why did she ever think she could talk to him? That he would be reasonable? And how did the police think he was a good samaritan?

"Do you want to see the block I used? I kept it. It still has her blood on it. Hold on. It's right here."

He took a step into the bedroom. Jessica wanted to get up and run, but he didn't go far enough that she could. By the time the thought entered her mind, he was back in front of her with Karli's brick. The red brick had been painted white and weathered. Karli treasured it. It came from the shed at her grandparents' house in Ohio. She spent hours working in there with her grandfather, and the brick was a leftover piece from the fire pit they built the summer before he died. She kept it with her as a reminder of him.

The man turned it to show Jessica the bloodstain that soaked into the porous surface. "See, right there? The blood just adds to the character of the piece. I love having something like this. It's like my old truck. Something that will always let me remember her. Even though our time together was far too short."

"Who told you to kill her?"

"Do you really think I'm going to tell you that?"

"Was it Damon? Was he trying to get to Raina?" Jessica asked. Maybe she could frazzle the man. Get him to admit something.

He straightened, his body stuttering just enough for it to be different. He shook his head and shrugged again. "I don't know what you're talking about."

"Yes, you do," Jessica argued. "It was Damon, wasn't it? He's the one behind all of this!"

"Shut up! You don't know what you're talking about!"

Jessica tried to get to her feet, but he shoved her back down. Her head hit the doorframe, and her vision spun. She refused to stay on the floor. To cower from him. She had to fight back. To find a way to get the truth out.

Jessica kicked at him and swung her arms. When he took a step back, she got her feet under her. He moved toward her again, and she grabbed for something, anything, she could use as a weapon. Her hand closed around something thin. She swung it, not knowing or caring what it was.

The umbrella she picked smacked into the doorframe opposite her. The man snorted and stepped on it, smashing her knuckles into the ground.

Jessica yelped and yanked her bruised and scraped fingers out from under the umbrella. He snickered again, but she moved around the doorframe and away from him, looking for anything she could use.

He chased her through the small space. She barely made it a few feet before he grabbed her hair.

If she couldn't fight him off, and she couldn't record what he said, she could draw attention to her presence.

She screamed. She poured all her energy into yelling out. "Ow! He's hurting me! Please help! Call the police!"

The man punched her in the stomach with the hand holding the brick, knocking the wind out of her and shutting her up.

Jessica doubled over, trying to catch her breath. She heaved air in, her insides screaming from the pain. A table was a few feet away. It looked heavy enough to make noise. If she couldn't make noise, she'd make sure his stuff made noise for her.

She lunged at the table and pushed it. It tipped, then paused, as if held by a string, then clattered to the floor.

"You bitch!" he hissed. "Stop it!"

She scrambled over the couch and flung a picture hanging on the wall toward him. He shouted when the corner of it caught him on the thigh.

Jessica was not going down without a fight. It was the fight of her life, and she wasn't done. She kicked and threw things. She raced around the apartment, trashing the place as she went. She was almost to the door when he grabbed her by the hair and yanked her backward.

Her back slammed to the floor, sending pain through every inch of her. All the air in her body burst from her, like a popped balloon. She tried to pull more air in, but her lungs were not having it. It hurt. Everything hurt. Her head spun, her body was bruised, she was almost out of fight.

"I wasn't planning to kill you, you know," he said, holding onto her hair while he dragged her away from the door. "I was going to let the police come and get you. Tell them they didn't protect my identity and the killer they were looking for showed up at my home. But I don't think I can do that now. You're fun."

"Fuck you," Jessica whispered. It hurt to speak and breathe and exist. The desire to let go was strong. To surrender to the darkness that wanted to drag her under and convince her it would be better if she just passed out.

But Jessica knew the things he would do to her if she couldn't fight him off. He told her. And she couldn't ever come back from that. If he forced himself on her, she'd rather be dead.

She had to keep fighting.

"We can do that, too. See, I told you. You're just like that first one. You want it, too."

"Not even if you were the last man alive. You're not a man. You're vile. You're a monster. The world will be a better place when you're dead."

He grinned. "You do get it. You get the desire. The drive. The pleasure that comes from ending a life. Oh, I wish I didn't have to kill you. I would have so much fun teaching you how beautiful it is to take a life. How horny it can make you. If you hadn't made so much noise, I might have been able to show you, but I don't know if anyone called the police, and I can't be caught fucking you. Killing you, sure, but not fucking you."

"You're not going to do either." Jessica's voice was rough and scratchy. Air ground across her vocal cords like sand.

"Oh, but I am. See, you're an intruder, and I have the right to defend myself and my property from a threat inside my home."

He held her hair in one hand and stretched with the other. When he straightened again, he had a knife and a smile.

"I'm going to enjoy this so much."

17

———

Jessica screamed as loud as she could. It hurt like hell. Her throat burned like she'd swallowed fire. But that was nothing compared to what she was sure the man would do.

"I feel like I should introduce myself," he said, yanking her hair back to meet her gaze. "I'm Silver. It's so nice to meet you, Ms. German. It'll be even nicer to kill you."

"You're not going to get away with this," she hissed.

He grinned wider and licked his teeth. He sucked in, baring his incisors like a rabid dog. "Why are you wearing this mask? Did you think it would hide who you are?"

Jessica had forgotten about the mask. When she put it on, she felt strong, powerful, invincible. Now, she just felt scared. Death was coming for her, and nothing was going to stop it. Not the mask or her strength or anything.

"This was a gift. From someone who knew what I was walking into."

Silver snickered. "They should have saved their money and told you not to come here instead. What did you think you were going to do? Beat me?"

"I am going to beat you," she growled.

Silver laughed. He paused and shook his head, then laughed harder. He laughed so hard he released her.

Jessica took advantage of the momentary freedom and pushed away from him. She scrambled to her feet and tried to find a way out. An escape.

"There's no escape," Silver said with a snort. "You're not leaving here unless it's in a body bag. You know too much."

"You're not going to get away with this. Not with killing Karli and not with the other woman you killed. You're going to jail."

"Nope. But thanks for asking."

He moved closer to her, cornering her by the kitchen. He was between her and the only escape. She looked around for another way out. There was a fire escape, but she didn't know how to get out onto it. Or if it was in good enough shape to get down it and away from him.

Silver lunged at her, swinging the blade in his hand while she was distracted. It caught her forearm, slicing into her flesh.

She cried out, clamping her other hand over it. The cut wasn't deep, but it was enough to sting. Before she could react, he swung again, cutting into her bicep.

Jessica needed a weapon. Something she could use to fight back. She yanked open a drawer, hoping to find something sharp. Or at least something solid to block his attacks.

The drawer was empty.

She moved back and pulled the next one. Towels. He watched her as she retreated farther into the apartment, yanking drawers and finding nothing useful. Even the brick he used to kill Karli would have been something, but she didn't know where he'd put it.

Silver laughed when Jessica got to the last drawer and

still came up empty. She moved around the island, finally seeing a path toward the door.

"Tsk, tsk. Did you really think it would be that easy?" he taunted as he hurried back to the other side of the island, once more blocking her exit.

"Aren't you worried about Raina's ex coming to get you? If I could find you, what makes you think he won't?"

"He's already been here," Silver admitted. Half a second later, he realized what he said. "Bitch."

Jessica filed the information away. "If he's looking for you, he'll be back."

"I'm not important enough for him to worry about right now. Not when he has bigger issues."

"Like what? What does he do?"

"Do you really think I'm going to tell you anything?"

"You already confessed he was the one who sent you after Karli. And he's after you now. And you told me about the first woman you raped and killed."

"Well, I guess it's a good thing you're not going to live long enough to tell anyone else what you know."

"I—"

Sirens screeched outside the window. Jessica paused, listening for them to draw closer. She was saved! The police would find them and arrest him for Karli's murder. And Jessica could tell him about everything else.

"Dammit!" Silver shouted. His eyes went wide, frantically scanning the room.

He moved away from Jessica, leaving space for her to escape. She moved toward the door, but he jumped back in front of her, blocking her again.

Jessica kicked him, surprising him with a swift blow to his knee. He went down with a shout, howling and holding his knee. She kicked his arm, a sickening crunch sounding above his shout before he grabbed for his arm.

"You fucking psycho!" he shouted. "What the hell is wrong with you?"

She wanted to laugh. He sliced and diced her and she was the psycho?

He tried to push to stand, but his knee gave out. He cursed and tried to use his arm, swearing again when it didn't support his attempt, either.

Footsteps echoed through the hallway outside the apartment. Before Jessica could do anything else, the door slammed open and police swarmed into the room.

Two officers went to Silver, and two went straight to her. Jessica put her hands up and opened her mouth, but Silver beat her to an explanation.

"Officers, thank God you're here. She broke into my apartment and tried to kill me. I managed to get the knife away from her and I cut her, but it was only because she was going to kill me like she did that nice lady who used to live across the hall from me. Please, help me."

"Liar!" Jessica shouted.

"Stop talking," one of the officers barked.

"Thank you, sir. You have to listen to me. He—"

"I said stop talking," the officers shouted. He twisted Jessica's arm behind her back and grabbed her other arm, dragging it to meet the first.

"Ow!"

"Jessica German. You're under arrest for the murder of Karli Sloane. You have the right to remain silent."

"What? I didn't kill her! He killed her. I came here because he's the one who called nine-one-one. He called before I was in her apartment. The only way he would have known she was dead was if he killed her. You have to believe me!"

The officers near Silver were looking at his arm. One radioed for an ambulance to treat his injuries.

"What about where he cut me? He said he was going to kill me. He killed another woman, too. His father went to jail for it, but he confessed to me."

"Shut up," the officer behind her said. He snapped cuffs on her wrists. "You have the right to an attorney."

"I don't want an attorney. I want you to listen to me. He killed my friend. He was going to kill me. Arrest him, not me!"

They all ignored her. The one officer continued to read Jessica her rights, and the others tended to Silver like he was a victim instead of the one they should be arresting.

Jessica wanted to scream at them. To get them to listen to her. To tell them they were arresting the wrong person. But instead, she was done. All the fight she had in her was gone. Running for weeks and fighting for her life and trying to prove her innocence had finally caught up to her, and she was just done.

Tears filled her eyes and overflowed onto her cheeks. She closed her eyes against the exhaustion and pain and frustration and just cried. She cried for Karli and Raina and Holly. She cried for herself. She cried for Braden and Taylor. She cried for the woman Silver killed when he was a teenager, and all the others he didn't tell her about. She just cried, letting it all out while the police officers stood there and ignored her, trusting the evil man who claimed to be a victim.

She would never be free again, but Silver would be. And Jessica would never forgive herself for not having proof of his crimes. For not getting justice for Karli.

BRADEN'S FOOT bounced as they drove through the streets toward Karli's building. He wasn't sure why there was a pit in his stomach, but he had a bad feeling about going there.

He still didn't know where Jessica was. He got a text from Stacey that she'd seen Jessica and Jessica was okay. She wouldn't tell him where she saw Jessica, or if Jessica said anything that would help him find her. It wasn't enough for Braden, but it was better than nothing.

They finally arrived at Karli's old building, and Braden jumped out with Wray. The call was for assistance for two people. One had lacerations that needed to be patched, and the other needed to go to the hospital for a more extensive evaluation. They were headed to Karli's floor, a few apartments down from hers, according to Wray.

"You okay?" Wray asked as they climbed the stairs.

Braden shook his head. "I want to be out there looking for her, not here. She's alone. And because the fucking cops won't do their fucking job and find the person who actually killed Karli, Jessica's out there somewhere."

"I get it," Wray said. "It was the same with Stacey. They questioned her for hours. And even now, she's convinced that Oscar dude didn't kill himself. She said his daughter was sure of it."

"Seriously?"

Wray nodded. "Yeah, but I keep telling her not to talk about that because she's the only suspect they have. They only let her go because they think it was a suicide."

"Stacey's not that person. I can't see her ever getting angry enough to kill someone."

"Jessica, too."

"Too bad PD doesn't think the same." Braden turned the

corner of the stairs and spotted four cops in the hallway. He exchanged a glance with Wray and moved toward the group.

"What's going on, gentlemen?" Wray asked.

"We finally caught the woman who killed her friend. She came back here when she found out this was the guy who called nine-one-one," one of the cops said.

Braden's blood went cold. Jessica. He turned his head, everything around him moving in slow motion. Jessica was inside the dirty apartment, her hands trapped behind her back and secured with handcuffs. Officer Shitface and Officer Dickwad were guarding her like she was going to be able to run.

Two other cops were talking to a man sitting on a dingy, stained couch. He was supporting his arm, which was bent at an awkward angle. His leg was straight out in front of him.

"Braden," Wray said, loudly. He smacked Braden's chest, bringing him back to reality.

Braden looked into the apartment again and caught Jessica's gaze. Her gaze was hollow, broken. Her shoulders were slumped. She was bloody and dirty and absolutely destroyed. And all Braden wanted to do was drag her out of there and hold her until it was all over.

"Jessica," Braden breathed. He rushed toward her, knowing Wray would handle the other patient.

Officer Dickwad stepped in front of Braden. "No."

"Fuck you. Move."

Office Shitface joined him. They crossed their arms and blocked Braden's path to Jessica. "This is an active crime scene."

"And I'm the fucking tooth fairy. What the fuck do you think we're doing here? We were called. And I'm going to treat her for her injuries. Or should I have some of your brothers in blue arrest you for denying her necessary medical treatment?"

The two officers exchanged a glance. Officer Dickwad stepped to the side with a grumble, barely giving Braden enough space to squeeze between them and reach Jessica.

"Are you okay?" he asked, opening his med kit.

She shook her head. "He killed Karli. He told me. He described the entire thing to me. But they don't want to hear it."

"He described it?" Braden asked. His heart flipped, and his gut churned. The sick son-of-a-bitch taunted her with the truth, and she just had to sit there and take it.

"I'm so sorry. And this is shitty timing, but I need you to know I did not call the police. I didn't turn you in. I never told them where the safe house was."

"I know. Stacey told me. I'm guessing Damon knew somehow. He must have been watching you. Or had Silver watching you. I don't know."

"Damon?"

Jessica nodded. "He told me Damon put him up to all of this. He said Damon hired him to kill Karli. But something went wrong because now Damon wants to kill him."

"Well, that's interesting news."

"I'm not sure how it helps me, though."

"It probably doesn't. Someone tried to kidnap Raina yesterday morning. She said she thought she recognized him from the building. I didn't think of it until now, but it could have been the same guy."

Jessica nodded. "I know. Stacey told me about that. He didn't admit it to me, but I figured it was him. Is Raina okay?"

"She's fine. As much as she can be. She fought him off. But he said something about letting two women get away, so he probably was following one of us and is the reason the cops found the safe house."

"This is all so messed up. And I was here. I was right here. I didn't record anything he said. The things he told me... He's sick Braden. He said he thinks he was put on earth to kill people."

Braden's gut clenched. Jessica was alone with the psycho. He could have walked into a very different scene. As much as he hated that the PD didn't do more to find the truth, he was grateful they showed up when they did and that Jessica only had a few lacerations on her arm and bruises on her body.

"Did he hurt you anywhere else?" Braden asked as he wrapped the second bandage on her arm. He'd cleaned the cuts, which thankfully weren't too deep, and held them together with bandages and covered the whole thing with gauze.

"Just dizzy and sore. He dragged me around by my hair and threw me on the floor. My back hurts like hell, and I probably have a concussion."

"Jesus," Braden breathed. He eyed the man who was playing up his injuries for Wray. Braden had half a mind to give him a few more. From what he could tell, the man deserved a whole lot worse than he got.

Jessica nodded. "God, Braden, I hate him. He even saved the brick he used to kill her. It was something Karli loved. A treasure from her grandfather."

"He saved it?"

"Yep. He showed it to me."

"Where is it? If it's here, it'll have Karli's DNA on it, and they can prove he killed her." Braden palpated Jessica's skull for tender spots where the killer tugged her hair too hard. She winced but didn't complain.

"I don't know where it is. When he got the knife, he must have put it somewhere."

"They should be trying to find it. They told me they don't have the murder weapon." Braden turned to the cops who were watching them carefully. "Hey, shit-for-brains. The brick the fucker used to kill Karli Sloane is somewhere in this apartment. How about you two do your damn jobs and fucking find it?"

"We're making sure she doesn't escape."

Braden snorted. "Really? She's in cuffs, and there are four officers in the hallway. You have that little faith in your coworkers that you think she's going to get past all of them?"

They exchanged another glance, then Officer Shitface walked toward the hallway.

Braden turned his focus back to Jessica. He looked into her eyes and held her gaze for a long minute. "I am so sorry you're going through all of this."

She nodded, her eyes watery. Her chin shook. She swallowed roughly.

"He's not going to get away with what he did. Now we know who he is and what he's capable of. Dex and his team will find out everything about him and make sure he never hurts anyone again."

"He's pure evil, Braden. He kills for fun. And if he's involved with Damon, there's no telling what else he's capable of. I didn't think I'd ever see you again."

"I'm right here, Jessica. I'm not going anywhere."

"I love you," she blurted.

Braden took a step back, instinct. He looked around, realizing everyone in the room heard her words. He opened his mouth to say something, anything, when Officer Shitface spoke.

"Well, what the hell is this?"

"What is that? I've never seen that before," the man Wray was tending to said. "Where did that come from?"

"Did you plant this in his apartment so he'd look guilty?" Officer Shitface asked Jessica.

Jessica looked past Braden to the officer, and her entire body sank like someone pulled a plug on a bounce house.

Braden turned and found the officer holding a brick and staring accusingly at Jessica.

"Glad we finally got the murder weapon," Officer Dickwad said. "Now, there's no way she'll get away with what she did."

Jessica sank to the floor and sobbed.

18

Jessica's gut burned like she'd swallowed fire. It consumed her, filling her with hot, blinding rage. As she cried, it built. Expanding from her stomach to her lungs and thighs, then to her throat and calves. When it reached her head and feet, she lost it.

"He killed Karli! She was my best friend in the world, and he took her away from me. He's a murderer. He killed before Karli. He ran a woman down on the side of the road and raped her, then let his own father take the blame for it and go to jail. He's the one who used that brick, a brick Karli saved from her childhood, to kill her. He told me how he waited until she'd been home a little while, then went into her apartment and smashed her on the back of the head. He wanted to rape her, too, but he thought he'd get caught. He's a monster."

"She's lying," Silver barked, his face twisted like he was in anguish. "I didn't know that woman across the hall. We said hi once or twice, but I had no reason to hate her. To kill her."

"He was hired to do it. Raina... Someone tried to kidnap

Raina yesterday morning. It was him. Call Marcus," Jessica breathed, turning to Braden. "Marcus can show Raina his picture. She can ID him."

Braden had his phone out by the time Jessica stopped talking.

"You can't do that," one of the officers said.

"The fuck I can't. Tell me why not? Captain Patrick is your boss. He might not be on Karli's case, but he's definitely involved with Raina's."

The officers shared a look. One of them stepped back toward the door, his gaze lingering on Silver.

Jessica felt a tiny sliver of hope. If they believed her, even just a little, there was a chance Silver wouldn't get away with everything he did. There was a chance they could prove he was the one who killed Karli. And then they could prove he was involved in however many other murders he committed.

"Marcus," Braden said, "are you at home? I need you to find Raina. I have a suspect here. Yes, I'm with him now. With Jessica." Braden looked at her, his eyes blazing with... something. "Okay, call me right back."

Jessica's hope started to falter. He didn't believe her.

"He's going to find Raina, then he'll call back with video so he can record it." Braden glared at Silver.

Silver paled, just slightly. He was still on the couch, complaining about his injuries. Wray had his arm stabilized and was working on his knee.

"I need to go to the hospital. Right now. I don't feel well. You've kept me here too long. I should already be in the hospital and safe from her. Instead, you've made me suffer in the same room as my attacker," Silver whined.

"Shut up," Wray snarled. "I'm giving you the best treatment possible. If you keep moving, you're going to make your injuries worse. And judging by the bruising on her face, you weren't the victim here."

Silver scowled at Wray, but fell silent when Braden's phone rang.

"Hey," Braden said.

"Raina is here. She's not going to speak, and she doesn't want him to see her."

"Understood. I'm going to flip my camera so you can see what I see instead of seeing me. I'll still be able to see you. Are you ready?"

Jessica watched the screen as Raina nodded. She offered Jessica a faint smile, and Jessica wished she could have done more.

Braden flipped the camera around, bringing Silver onto the screen. Silver immediately ducked, slithering down the couch like the snake he was.

"I don't consent to having my image recorded," Silver barked.

"Get his ass up," Braden snapped. "He doesn't get to choose that when he's a suspect."

To Jessica's relief, the other cops moved toward Silver and lifted him. They turned him around so his face was in full view of the camera.

Raina gasped. She looked up at Marcus and nodded.

"We have a positive identification. Who's there with you?" Marcus said.

"Officers Maxwell and Dempsey," Braden growled.

"Officers. Detain that man for attempted kidnapping. I'll be in touch with Lieutenant Juarez about the rest. We'll meet you, all of you, at the station," Marcus demanded.

The officers nodded, and Braden told Marcus they agreed to his request.

Braden switched the camera back around so Marcus

could see him. "Thank you. He had the murder weapon. He said Jessica planted it in his apartment."

"We'll get it all straightened out. But Jessica needs to come to the station, too. She's still a suspect until we can prove he's the one we should have been after all this time."

Braden looked up at her and met her gaze. She wanted to cry again, but she still had a fight. A fight that was almost over. One that meant she would finally be free.

AT THE POLICE STATION, Jessica was shown into an interrogation room and cuffed to the table. Her arm hurt from the cuts, and she was so tired she almost fell asleep, but she had hope that it would all be over soon now that Marcus was involved, even just a little.

Marcus talked to her when she arrived and asked how she was. He said he wouldn't be involved in questioning her, but he was going to make sure she was okay. That was the best news she'd heard in weeks.

When the door finally opened, a tall man with dark hair and brown skin walked in. He was followed by one of the officers from Silver's apartment.

"Ms. German," the first man said. "You've given us quite a chase."

Jessica didn't reply. Agreeing would have incriminated herself and confirmed that she knew the police were looking for her. Even though everyone in the room knew that was the truth, Jessica wasn't going to admit it.

"My officer here said you made some pretty pointed accusations against the man you attacked." His shirt said Juarez, and Jessica remembered that was the name of the lieutenant Marcus was going to talk to. He was in charge of Karli's case.

"Silver told me he killed Karli."

"Why were you at his apartment?"

"I received a message through social media with a recording of the nine-one-one call. He said his address."

"So, you thought you'd tie up loose ends?" Juarez asked.

"No! I wanted to know why he said I killed Karli. I was in her apartment when I called nine-one-one, and the operator said someone had already called it in. The only way he would have known she was dead was if he killed her."

"What were you going to do?"

"I wanted the truth. I wanted to know why my friend was dead. She was a good person. She was kind and caring. She loved her job, and she was a good friend. She didn't deserve to die."

"Let me get this right. You went to his apartment, wearing a mask, so you could talk to the man?" Juarez asked.

Jessica nodded. She understood it didn't look good, but it was the truth. All she was after was the truth. Karli deserved that much.

Jessica shifted, the cuffs tugging at her wrists and pulling on the slices on her arms. She didn't bother to complain, but she shifted again to alleviate the pain.

"A friend gave me the mask. Said it would make me feel confident. She knew what I was walking in to. And—"

"Someone knew you were going there and didn't call it in?" the other officer blurted.

Jessica shook her head, wincing at the dizziness the movement caused. Braden said she likely had a concussion, but there was nothing that could be done to speed up the healing. His advice was to rest, but that wasn't an option.

"She didn't know where I was going. She knew I was

going to talk to someone, and that I thought I'd figured out who'd killed Karli, but she didn't know who it was. I didn't tell her."

"Who was this person?" Lieutenant Juarez asked.

"When do I get a lawyer?"

Lieutenant Juarez leaned back in his seat. "You haven't asked for one."

"I am now. I'd like a lawyer, please."

The officer from the scene rolled his eyes, but Lieutenant Juarez simply stood and nodded. They left the room, leaving Jessica alone again.

Maybe now someone would listen to her.

"WHAT'S GOING ON?" Braden asked Marcus. He had to report back for the rest of his shift, but as soon as he was off duty, he went to the police station to get Jessica.

And found her still in custody.

"Lieutenant Juarez questioned her, but she asked for a lawyer."

"I'll call Taylor," Braden said.

"I already got her one. He's the best criminal defense attorney in town."

Braden opened his mouth to say something, but Marcus held up his hand.

"Because he's good at what he does and he's not crooked. He has no ties to any criminal organization. He only works with individuals. He never takes on cases for big companies."

"How does he get paid?" Braden asked.

"I don't ask. But he's good. The best. I called him because I knew he'd be the best option for Jessica."

"Thank you," Braden breathed. "She needs some support right now."

Marcus nodded. "The guy they brought in with her?"

Braden nodded in understanding.

"His DNA matched the DNA on Raina's clothes. He was definitely the one who tried to kidnap her."

"Have you spoken to him yet?"

Marcus shook his head. "No. We're waiting on the results from the brick. We want to be able to go at him with both things."

"Does that mean they believe Jessica now?"

"It means they're more open to the possibility. Juarez is a reasonable person, but he had no choice but to follow the evidence. The video he had first was the one that showed the calls came in after Jessica left. There were a lot of things stacked against her. I would have proceeded the same way if I didn't know her."

"You never would have thought she did this."

"No, but that's why I wasn't on the case. You know how it is when personal feelings get in the way of doing your job."

Braden nodded slowly, thinking about walking away from Jessica earlier. He didn't want to leave her side. He wanted to stay with her. But if he had, he would have lost his job. It killed him to walk away, but he did it.

And regretted it every second.

"If they prove this Silver guy killed Karli, what's going to happen to Jessica?"

Marcus shrugged. "That's going to be up to Juarez. But her lawyer will argue that she should be released since she did nothing wrong. She didn't resist arrest or attack anyone. The worst they could do would be obstruction of justice, but even that wouldn't hold up if she's no longer a suspect."

"So, she might be done?"

"Maybe. I can't guarantee that."

"But it's possible."

Marcus nodded. "It's possible."

"Thank God."

"I AM SO sorry you're in the middle of this mess, Ms. German. Marcus called me and explained everything. I will get you out of here and get all of this erased for you. I'm Gage Stevens, by the way, your attorney. We haven't met."

Gage Stevens was a force. He walked into the room looking like a man with power and confidence and strength Jessica had never possessed. She liked him on sight, even more when he smiled kindly at her and closed the door in the face of the officer who escorted him to her interrogation room.

"Marcus called you?" Jessica asked.

Gage nodded. "We're old friends. He knows I take on cases like yours. I have to ask, because I ask all my clients, are you guilty of what they're trying to accuse you of?"

Jessica shook her head. "Karli Sloane was my best friend. I was going to her apartment to talk about a date I had the night before. I brought pizza. She was dead when I got there, and I panicked."

"Good. Not that you panicked, but that you're innocent. And panicking in a situation like that is completely normal. If you hadn't panicked, I'd be a little worried about you." He laughed, his eyes crinkling on the sides. He was an attractive man. Dark skin and eyes with short, dark hair. His teeth were slightly crooked in the front, but it added to his charm and made him more approachable and personable.

"What do we do now?"

"You sit tight. I'm going to argue that there's no reason to hold you since you haven't been charged with anything and you've been through hell. Is it true the man who actually killed your friend is the one whose apartment you were in?"

Jessica nodded, her cheeks warming at the admission. "I got a message with the nine-one-one call. The full recording, which I hadn't heard before. He said his address. I wanted to know why he said he saw me running from Karli's apartment."

"Did you?"

"Did I what?"

"Did you run?"

"Yes, but not until after he called, after I called. The operator I spoke to said the police were already on the way when I called. That's why I ran."

"And the police didn't line all this up?"

"They had video that was tampered with, I guess. He told me he gave it to them so they would believe his story."

"He sounds smart. A whole lot smarter than he appears to be."

Jessica nodded. "He's evil. He's killed others. He shouldn't be free." She shivered at the memory of the things he shared.

Gage watched her closely for a moment, then nodded. "Thank you, Ms. German. I will make sure he isn't set free. And that you are."

"Thank you."

Gage squeezed her shoulder, then walked out of the room.

Jessica wondered how long she would have to sit there, but knowing someone was on her side made the whole thing easier. Someone believed her. She'd get her freedom.

DAMON STARED at the report on his phone in the backseat of the SUV. He tied up all the loose ends with the shipment and was heading back to the office when a text came in with a link to the news report.

`Local woman captured. Accomplice in custody.`

Damon swore as he read the short article beneath the video. Jessica found Silver. Not only that, but she had enough on him to get Silver arrested, too. Which meant it was only a matter of time before the man made a deal to get away with murder. Literally.

Damon glanced at his driver. The new, new guy. The last new guy didn't come back after Damon put a gun to his head. No fucking loyalty. He was paid for his service and would never tell anyone who he worked for. Dead men didn't talk.

The old driver Damon had was a man he could say anything in front of and know it would never go anywhere. He proved his loyalty time and again. When he decided to retire and leave the area, Damon agreed on the condition the man never told anyone what he used to do or who he worked for. When he assured Damon he wouldn't, Damon trusted the man and let him go.

But the newest one was still a wildcard. Better than the last, but not as good as the old one. Damon had hope, though. So far, he hadn't questioned Damon.

"I need to go to the office," Damon barked at the driver.

Time was running out. If the article was already published, it was possible it was too late, but Damon couldn't risk anything getting out. He had to take care of the threat.

The driver pulled up in front of the office a few minutes later and turned off the vehicle.

"Keep it running. I'll be back in a minute," Damon said.

The driver nodded and cranked the SUV back up. He was learning. He must have figured out loyalty was the only way to keep the job, and his life.

Damon stalked through the warehouse and into his office. Mick followed behind him, guarding Damon's movements. Mick stayed outside the office, watching the door while Damon sat behind his desk.

He lifted the receiver on his desk, one he always used and knew couldn't be traced.

"Yeah?" the voice on the other end of the line said.

"You have a suspect in custody. Silver James. He knows too much. He needs to be taken care of. Immediately."

"Yes, sir," the voice said.

The line went dead.

Silver would be next.

19

———

"You're free to go," Marcus said as he opened the door to the room Jessica had been in for hours.

She had no idea how much time had passed, but it didn't matter. She was free. "Free? Like I can walk out of here and no one is going to chase me? You're not sneaking me out, are you?"

Marcus breathed a laugh and shook his head. "No illegal stuff going on. You're free, Jessica. And you helped us bring in a killer."

"He really did it. He really killed her, didn't he?"

Marcus nodded. "He did. The DNA on the brick matched Karli's from her autopsy and Silver's. There was another DNA that isn't in our system, but it didn't match you, so there's no way to tie you to it."

"Maybe it was Raina's?" Jessica said.

"That's what I figured, too. It doesn't really matter, though. It's all the proof we need that he—"

"Call nine-one-one!" someone shouted down the hallway.

Jessica and Marcus looked at each other, then moved

into the hallway together. Marcus looked to where the officers were rushing and followed them. Jessica wasn't sure where she was supposed to go, so she went with him, hanging back to stay out of the way.

"He's not breathing," someone said.

"Someone start CPR."

"What the hell happened?"

Jessica reached the door and saw Silver slumped over in his seat. Drool pooled on his face and down to his shirt. His color was even paler than the last time she saw him. Gray. Ashy. Dead.

The officers removed his cuffs and laid him on the floor. One of them started CPR, pressing on Silver's chest.

Jessica felt like she was in a trance, staring as the man's lifeless body jerked and twitched with the futile efforts of the officer. A minute later, someone bumped her to the side and hurried into the room.

The new person told the officer to stop for a vitals check. He set two fingers on Silver's throat, like Jessica had done to Karli weeks ago. A few seconds later, the man shook his head. "He's dead."

"How the fuck did this happen?" someone in the room barked.

Jessica moved to see who it was and found Lieutenant Juarez staring at the body.

"He's been in our custody for hours. No one has been in here to see him. How is he dead?"

"He has a water bottle," Marcus said. "Someone could have put something in it."

"Those bottles come from the station storage. It had to be signed out. Who the hell gave him the water?"

"I did, sir," an officer Jessica didn't recognize said.

"Why did you give him water?"

"He asked. I've done it for people tons of times. I didn't know it would be an issue."

"Did you tamper with it?"

"No, sir. I don't know what happened."

"This is not good. Had anyone questioned him?" Juarez asked. His gaze found Marcus.

"I was coming in here next. Right after you."

"Fuck!" Juarez shouted. "We had him. We had the killer. And instead of being able to tell the city he's behind bars, we have to tell the city he's dead. Someone's ass is on the line for this. We need to find out who got to him and how."

"Damon," Jessica breathed. She didn't know how he did it, but she had no doubt he did. She stepped forward. "Someone was after him. When I got to his apartment, he thought I was there to kill him. Damon was after him. He's the one who hired him."

"Who the hell is Damon?" Juarez asked.

"My CI's ex. I'll talk to her. See if I can get her to sit down with a sketch artist. He seems to be the one behind all of this." Marcus leveled Juarez with a look that said he was on it.

"Thank you, sir. I apologize for losing my temper." Juarez glanced at Jessica and nodded.

"What happened?" Braden asked from behind her.

"What are you doing here?" Jessica blurted.

"I came to get you. What's going on?"

"Silver's dead," Jessica told him.

"What?"

"He's dead. He won't sit in jail for the rest of his life and think about all the people he hurt. Of course, the bigger punishment for him might have been not being able to hurt more people. The world is a better place without him in it."

"You can't say things like that here," Braden whispered.

Jessica rubbed her hands up and down her arms and nodded. She stepped to the side while the officers in the room with Silver taped off the door and called the medical examiner.

"Are you ready to leave?"

Jessica nodded. "I am. I'm free. I just need to figure out where I'm going to go from here."

"For tonight, Taylor wants us to come to her place. And after that, I'm hoping I can talk you into staying in Niagara Falls. Maybe even staying with me."

"I don't know Braden—"

"I love you," he blurted. "I should have said it when you did before, but I kind of panicked. You surprised me, and I felt the same thing, but I wasn't expecting you to say it when you did. And I wanted to tell you when there were a few less witnesses. And when you weren't in handcuffs. But I love you. I want you with me. In my life, in my house, in my bed. Forever, Jessica. I don't want you to leave Niagara Falls."

Tears streamed down her cheeks as he spoke. She nodded, unable to push the words out.

"Yes? You'll stay?"

"All of it," she breathed.

Braden wrapped his arms around her waist and pulled her in close. "So, I'll get you at work and at home?"

"At work? What are you talking about?"

"I quit my job today," Braden said.

"What? You can't do that."

"I already did."

"Why? Why would you quit your job?"

"Because I had to leave you today. You were hurt and getting arrested, and I had to go back to work instead of having the freedom to go with you."

"I can't let you do that, Braden. I can't let you give up something you love so much."

"I'm not. I'm choosing someone I love more. I've always seen the world as black and white. Good and bad. Right and wrong. I couldn't see the messy middle. The gray that most people lived in. Not until these last two weeks with you. There is no more black and white for me. There's only you. And I know you are always going to be on the side of good."

"Braden..."

"Leaving that job was the right choice. So many times over the last two weeks I've wanted to walk away, but I didn't have the courage to do it. You've shown me courage isn't something we have. It's something we have to fight for. Backing down to toe a line isn't the answer. Standing up and fighting for the people who can't fight for themselves is what we all need to do more of."

"God, I love you. You're amazing. Even if I think it's going to cost you more than you think."

He leaned down and kissed her. "It won't cost me you. That's what matters to me. If I have you, I'm good. Besides, Taylor has been asking me to work security for her for years."

"That's what you meant by that?" Jessica asked with a laugh.

Braden nodded. "I think it's a great plan. She can't say no to me."

"Who could?"

Taylor hugged Jessica so tight she almost cracked a rib. "I'm so happy you're safe. And free. And that my brother finally realized how amazing you are."

Taylor winked at Braden, who had yet to let Jessica get farther away than an arm's length. They were in Taylor's backyard, surrounded by Dex and his team and their families, but Braden wasn't straying far.

"Me, too. On all of it," Jessica said.

Taylor smiled brightly. Jessica could see the worry and the exhaustion on her friend's face and hated that she put Taylor through so much over the last few weeks.

"How are you? Are you doing okay?"

Taylor snorted. "I'm fine. Just terrified. I thought someone would find you or something would happen. I was so mad at Dex for not telling me where you were all the time. He said they were on it, but he knew if I knew, I'd go see you and put you at risk."

"Thank you for having them watch out for me. It was scary to be out there alone. And to not know if I'd ever be able to come back."

"I would have dragged you back here if you tried to leave. I can't do all of this without you."

"You would have figured it out. You didn't stop everything while I was gone."

"I almost did. I never realized how much you keep running for me. I owe you a big raise."

"No, you don't."

"I do. But we can argue about that another time. Can I ask how things are with my brother?" Taylor dropped her voice low.

"No, you can not," Braden said, stepping forward and wrapping his arm around Jessica.

Jessica chuckled, but she was not going to complain. "I guess we'll have to talk at work."

"Where I'll also be. All the time."

"You're not going to let me have any girl talk with my friend?" Taylor pouted.

"I will. As long as it's not about me," Braden argued.

"You're no fun."

"I know. Now, I think Jessica and I need to go. It's been a long few weeks for her."

Taylor stepped forward and hugged Jessica tight. "I am so happy you're safe."

"Me, too."

They said their goodbyes and Braden drove them back to his place. Her apartment was no longer under the control of the police, but Jessica wasn't ready to go back there yet. She wasn't sure when she would be. Braden offered to move all her stuff out and into his place, but Jessica was still deciding what she wanted to do. Moving in with Braden after only a few weeks and one official date felt way too fast. Even if it also felt way too right.

They curled up on the couch together, like a regular couple who hadn't been through hell over the last few weeks. Braden stroked her hair and kissed the top of her head.

"You know, I really do want you to move in. I know it's fast, but you're it for me."

"I'm it for you?" she asked.

He nodded, shifting to look at her. Jessica sat up and turned toward him. "The first day I saw you, I thought you were the most beautiful woman in the world. You ran into the glass door, and I thought you were adorable. And a little clumsy."

"You saw that?" Jessica buried her face in her hands.

He pulled her hands apart. When she looked up at him, he nodded. "I did. And I still thought you were beautiful. But I wouldn't let myself see you as a possibility. I put you in a Do Not Touch box and taped it shut. Taylor kept saying things about you over the years and picking at that tape until she pried the box open, and I found myself unable to resist you. Our date... I've never enjoyed a date that much in my life. And I knew I'd regret it if I didn't invite you back here. It wasn't pre-planned, but I couldn't stop myself from wanting more of you once I had a little taste. And I still feel that way. I know it's only been a few weeks, but you mean everything to me. I want you here day and night with me. Whenever you're ready."

"It feels soon," Jessica admitted.

Braden nodded. "It does, but it feels right."

She breathed a laugh. "It does."

"So, you'll move in with me. Stay here?"

Jessica nodded. "Yes. I will."

"Good. Then I think it's time for bed."

He bent over and scooped her up and carried her to bed.

JESSICA WAS STILL SMILING the next morning when she rang Stacey's doorbell. They were meeting with Raina and Frannie to talk about Damon and Karli and everything that had happened. Frannie didn't want to meet at the shelter and risk scaring any of the other women, so they chose Stacey's house.

Stacey hugged Jessica when she let her in and asked how she was doing.

"Good," Jessica said, once again unable to hide her smile.

Stacey snorted. "I know that grin. That's the grin of a woman who's in love."

"That's the grin of a woman who had a lot of sex," Frannie added.

"Both," Jessica admitted.

"Good for you," Raina said. "I'm so happy you and Braden were able to be okay through all of this. I hope one day we can have that girl talk we were supposed to have with Karli."

Jessica nodded, her joy fading slightly at the reminder of everything they'd all been through and everything they were still going through. Raina wasn't safe. Her ex was still out there, and he'd already killed at least two people to try to get to her.

"How are you holding up?" Jessica asked Raina.

Raina shrugged. "As well as I can expect. I wish Damon would go away. I'll never go back to him. But he's sick and doesn't understand that."

"You're strong," Frannie said. "Keep that spirit. You're going to need it with a man like him."

Raina nodded. "I know. I just wish I never moved in with Karli. I hate that she paid the price for my poor choice in men."

"You didn't know he was going to turn out to be so horrible," Jessica defended. "Karli wanted you to be safe. She wanted you to have a life. We have to choose to go on living and fighting for what's right. That's what she would have wanted."

Raina reached across the table and squeezed Jessica's hand. "You're right. That's exactly what she would have wanted. I was so scared that day when I got to the building and saw all the police cars. I just kept going, not slowing down to look. I knew it didn't matter what had happened, it was bad. I've been hiding since, but Damon still found me. The only way this is all going to end is if he's dead or in jail."

"Let's go for jail," Frannie said with a twinkle in her eye and a wink.

"Okay, we'll go for that," Raina said. She smiled.

"So, how are we going to find him?" Stacey asked. "He seems to be the one behind all of this. Even if the police are looking, they don't have much to go on."

The doorbell rang before anyone could say anything else. Stacey looked at the others, her brows pulled together.

"Are you expecting anyone else?" Frannie asked.

Stacey shook her head and left to answer the door.

Jessica and the others watched the front, waiting for Stacey and not wanting to say anything without her there. They heard the door open and Stacey gasp.

"Oh, my God. How are you here?"

Jessica looked at the others, but none of them moved.

The person answered, but their voice was too soft for Jessica to hear what they said.

"Come back here. Now. Jessica, Raina, and Frannie are here."

"I know," the voice said, closer now. A voice Jessica never thought she'd hear again. "That's why I came."

"Karli?" Jessica and Raina said at the same time.

Karli stepped into the kitchen. Alive. Upright.

"How are you here?" Frannie asked. "We thought you were dead."

"So did whoever thought they killed me. That's why I've been hiding."

"He's dead. Jessica found him. Damon was behind it all."

"I know. What I don't know is who it was that they killed. But she wasn't supposed to be there. She broke in."

"What?" Jessica asked.

"You saw her?" Raina asked.

Karli nodded. "I saw her. And she looked just like me. I

have no idea who she was or why she was in my apartment, but I need to find out."

Everyone deserves justice. Even when they're no one.

Witnessing a murder was not on Frannie's bucket list.
Marcus had to find out what the curvy dancer knew.
They made a deal. She would help him, and he would find the murderers. No one would know she was involved. She hoped.

Frannie and Marcus's story is available only to subscribers.
Sign up at https://dl.bookfunnel.com/y9ms2k2dq8 to get FORSAKEN now.

FEIGN IS COMING NOVEMBER 18…

Everyone thinks Karli Sloane is dead. In order to stay alive, she has to keep it that way. But someone is dead. The woman who broke into Karli's apartment took her place unintentionally. Karli needs to know who she was and why she was there. And Cade might be the only one with the answers. If he can get her to trust him.

Preorder FEIGN today!

CHAPTER ONE

Taylor Wright caressed the multicolored bow on the box with a satisfied smile. She'd been getting gifts from supporters and investors for weeks, each more lavish and thoughtful than the last.

After years of killing herself to make it to the top, she'd finally arrived. She was doing exactly what she wanted to do, and she was doing it exactly how she wanted to do it.

She had her enemies, but they were people she'd left behind her. People she wasn't interested in involving in her success. She'd built her company from the ground up and she was going to open up to customers in two weeks. Initial reviews were overwhelmingly positive, proving she was doing things right.

Taylor lifted the lid with a curious smile on her face. She peered inside and screamed, "Gah!" She dropped the lid and backed away from it. Cement filled her gut and ice flooded her veins.

"Are you okay? What happened?" her assistant Jessica's near-permanent grin faded to confusion when she saw the panicked look in Taylor's eyes.

The only thing Taylor could do was point to the box. Jessica turned to it, then back to Taylor with narrowed eyes and a tilt of her head that assumed Taylor was being dramatic and crazy.

Jessica had worked for Taylor for almost a year. She was the closest thing Taylor had to a friend, even though they really weren't friends, but Taylor thought her assistant had a little more trust in her than to think she was nuts.

"What—? Oh, my God. Is that what I think it is?"

"If you think it's a dead bird nestled in decaying roses with a note that reads *you're next*, then yes, it's what you think it is."

"Who the hell would send you something like that?"

"Someone who wants us to fail."

"Okay, but who?"

Taylor shook her head. "I have no idea."

"I'll send you the list, officer," Taylor said for the third time in thirty minutes. "I want to be thorough."

"Does the bird have any significance?" the young cop asked.

Taylor fought the urge to roll her eyes. She was exhausted. It had been a long day before she walked into her office and found a dead bird in a box. She glanced around at the walls, covered in birds. "Yeah, the bird is significant."

Taylor called her company Birds of a Feather because she wanted the women she targeted to know they weren't alone. It was important to her since Taylor herself never felt like she connected with the women she knew, but she hoped to create a world where other women didn't feel the same.

Birds of a Feather was more than a company to her. It was her baby. Her dream when she was in grad school and imagining her future, a future she thought she would share with her boyfriend. Mark was ambitious and studious, just like Taylor, but what she couldn't see at the time was that he was also jealous of her creativity and lacked his own.

It didn't bother Taylor, but it was a sore spot for Mark. So sore that he stole an idea he and Taylor came up with together and pitched it as his own to get himself a job at the company where they both first interviewed. When Taylor pitched the same idea, as a joint venture, they all but accused her of stealing it and said the only reason they weren't reporting her to the school was because they knew the truth.

That was when Taylor learned not to trust other people. Especially men.

"Do any men work here?" the officer asked, dragging Taylor's focus back to the issue in front of her.

Again, she had to resist an eye roll. "Birds of a Feather is an inclusive work environment. We hire the person who is best for the job, but when developing a company of size inclusive exercise clothes for women, it attracts more women than men."

The officer stared at the rear end of one of the interns as she rushed past Taylor's office. Sure, she was cute and perky and perfect, but the man was on the damn job.

"Ahem," Taylor said loudly.

The cop almost dropped his notepad as he yanked his eyes from the woman's ass. Minor victories.

He pressed his lips together in what she assumed was supposed to be a smile and gave Taylor and her ample curves a dismissive once-over before announcing, "I think I have all I need. If we find anything, we'll be in touch, Ms...."

"Wright," Taylor provided.

"Yes, of course." He picked up the evidence bag containing the box and nodded, then left her office.

Taylor's sigh was more of a groan as she scolded herself that flipping off a cop was not in her best interest, just in case he turned around and caught her.

She watched until he made it to the bank of elevators, then sank into her chair. She was drained. Dealing with threats and cops could do that to a woman.

"What did he say?" Jessica was another one the cop admired on his way to see Taylor. She had jet black hair, a curvy hourglass figure, and a smile that would make any man drop to his knees and beg for her to flash it at him, but Taylor hired her because she was also crazy smart and could think quickly on her feet. She'd saved Taylor's ass more than once in the last year.

"He said they'll be in touch."

"Which means we'll never see him again."

"Yep. Whatever."

"Why don't you call Braden?" Jessica suggested.

Taylor took note of the way Jessica's voice lifted at the end, as though there was more than one reason she might want Taylor's brother aware of what was going on. Taylor resisted the urge to call either of her brothers about anything, but Braden was the worst. He was the worrier. The one who was always telling her she needed to be more careful. Being a firefighter, he saw some of the worst the world had to offer, but he was paranoid. And Taylor wasn't going to be afraid to live her life.

"I don't think I need to tell Braden about this."

"Tell me about what?" Braden asked from Taylor's doorway.

Taylor sighed and gave Jessica a look that asked if she set Taylor up. Jessica flushed fifty shades of pink and tucked her hair behind her ear before she hurried out of the office, sneaking past an oblivious Braden on her way back to her desk. Braden's gaze followed her for half a second, then snapped back to his sister. "What happened?"

"It was nothing."

"Then why did I pass Officer Shaw on my way up here?"

"Dammit," Taylor hissed.

"What happened?"

"Just someone being an ass."

"Which means?"

"I got a dead bird in the mail. Wrapped up in a pretty box and nestled in a bed of decaying roses." Taylor delivered the words with a pissed-off smile that hid the threat of showing her brother what she had for lunch.

"What?" Braden stalked across the room to her side. His fists clenched, and he twisted his neck to release the tension that immediately locked it up.

Taylor shrugged like the whole thing was a minor inconvenience instead of a not-so-thinly veiled threat to everything she'd worked her ass off to build. That was exactly why she didn't want to tell him. And why she didn't mention the note.

"You need protection, Tay. Someone with you to make sure you're safe."

"No," Taylor said. Now that was why she didn't want to tell him. The last thing she wanted was to feel like a prisoner in her own life.

"Taylor—"

"Would you be telling Aaron this? Or Wray or one of your other firefighter buddies? Is it because I'm a woman?"

"It's because you're my sister, Tay-tay. I don't want anything to happen to you."

Taylor's frozen heart melted whenever he called her by her childhood nickname. Especially when he tilted his head to the side and gave her the same lost little boy look he'd worn on a daily basis growing up. As the oldest of four, Taylor took a mother role with her younger siblings. She started babysitting them when she was able to use the microwave for dinner, and she was changing Braden's diapers, the youngest, the day he came home from the hospital. Taylor's greatest accomplishments were her siblings.

Until Birds of a Feather.

"I'll be fine," she assured Braden. "Whoever sent it is just trying to scare me."

"Which is exactly my point. I know a guy—"

"Don't go there, Braden." Taylor's sharp look and sharper tone would have made most people shut up quickly, but he was her brother and knew she was like a chihuahua pretending to be a Great Dane.

His matching glare had the punch of a pissed off hornet, but she wouldn't tell him that. "Taylor."

"Braden."

"I'm worried about you."

Taylor shook her head to dislodge the equally powerful sting of his soft words. "I have the best security system money can buy, both here and at home. There are cameras all over this building. I have no reason to think this is anything more than some sick joke, but if it's not, I have a baseball bat under my bed and you know I can swing it."

Braden's entire face softened at the mention of their shared memories. One of the many roles Taylor took on was coaching his baseball team when he was seven. She'd just turned eighteen and knew little about the game, but she learned fast. Just like she did with everything else in her life.

"At least meet the guy. Talk to him."

"Braden."

"Taylor, please. It'll make me feel better if you have a conversation with him."

"Let me think about it."

Braden's sigh was his annoyed sigh, the one that Taylor had grown accustomed to him using on her since he realized he was finally bigger and stronger than his big sister, and that she still wouldn't let him take care of her. "I guess that's all I can hope for."

Taylor's grin bordered on a smirk. "Yep."

Ryker Hamilton sat in the briefing room and listened to his boss talk about their latest job. Ryker, known as Dex to the rest of the team, had taken his turn as lead on a few cases, but he was happy when Dunn filled the role. It was natural for him, but Dex… he liked to be behind the scenes most of the time. He was comfortable being in second place.

"Dex, are you with us?" Dunn asked.

Dex nodded, meeting the gaze of the other man. It didn't matter what the task was, Dex was up to it. F-BOMB was as much his baby as the others'. They'd built the company from the ground up over the last few years, working to protect the borders of their country and keep people safe. That included stopping all sorts of bad guys, and brought them to their current asshole.

Dennis Parker.

Parker was the kind of scum that gave scum a bad name. He was involved in anything and everything bad. But he was smart enough to stay a step or two away from it and never get his hands dirty.

Dex hated men like him because everyone knew they were the ones pulling the strings, but their puppets always protected them. It wasn't because of loyalty, though. He had something on everyone who'd ever worked for him. And he wasn't afraid to use it to ruin their lives if they ever thought about ruining his.

"How are we going to handle this?" Archer asked.

Archer was their smash and grab guy. He could tear someone apart with his bare hands if he needed to. He was a good man to have on your side, and he was smarter than he gave himself credit for.

"The sheriff is out for blood. We have to bring the entire organization down," Dunn said. He met the gazes of the rest of the team with his own dark one.

"And we're sure it was one of Parker's men who took the sheriff's daughter and did that to her?" Rocky winced at the picture of the bruised woman on their board. He was the rational one of the group. Rocky thought through their actions and made a decision long before he acted.

"We're sure," Dunn said. "The guy bragged to her about other cases they've been tied to. He knew too much to be spouting rumors. He was a part of it."

"What's the play here?" Dex asked. "Normally, the powers that be would bring in someone like this guy and cut him a deal in order to get his boss. I can't imagine that's the plan with this one."

"No, it's not. We want to take down the entire organization. To do that, we need to know what he has on his people," Dunn said. "We need his files."

"Where do we think they are?" Jack asked.

"They're not digital," English said. As the team's computer expert, if something existed online, English would find it. A self-professed nerd, English was the kind of guy who could shoot you with one hand and ruin you with the other. He was as badass as they came, but he stayed in the shadows more often than not.

"That means everything is on paper. Files somewhere. Probably more than one copy if he's smart, and we know he is. I'd be willing to bet he has a copy at his home, one in the office, and another somewhere that we don't know about," Dunn said.

The frustration in Dunn's voice matched that of the rest of the group. It wasn't that they were simply frustrated that they couldn't bring the guy down, they were frustrated that he impressed them. Not in a way that made them want to be like him, but in a way that made them wonder how he pulled it all off without being caught. After everything they'd seen, not much got past them, but Parker did. More than once.

Dex's phone rang, prompting a pause to the meeting. He looked up at Dunn for permission to answer during the meeting. Dunn nodded.

"Hamilton."

"Ryker, this is Braden Wright. I wondered if I could call in that favor."

Dex waved off Dunn's look to let him know it wasn't anything relevant to the current case, then left the conference room to talk to Braden. After Braden went undercover with Dex and saved his life at an illegal poker game a few months earlier, Dex vowed to return the favor anytime Braden needed something.

"Everything okay?"

"That's why I'm calling. My sister is about to launch her newest company and she's getting threats. Most have been stupid online things, but the latest was a dead bird. Do you have time to act as private security for her? A few weeks, maybe?"

"For you, Braden, anything."

"Thanks. I owe my sister everything, and she doesn't like to admit when she needs help."

"I've met a few people like that."

Braden chuckled. "Yeah, well, she did raise me. I'll send you her company's address. You're on her calendar for tomorrow afternoon. Thanks, Ryker."

"Any time. We'll talk soon."

Braden hung up, and Dex went back into the conference room. Dunn raised a brow at him, pausing his sentence just long enough for Dex to nod in response to the unasked question. *Everything is fine.*

"So," Dunn said, "how are we going to bring this asshole down?"

Everyone had left for the day, but Taylor still sat at her desk. She refused to leave anything to chance this close to her launch. Years of working jobs that made ends meet had led her to where she was. On top of the damn world.

She checked and double checked her notes and confirmed everything with her suppliers and manufacturer. She'd thought of everything, except sabotage.

Taylor tried to come up with a list of people who might be out to get her, but she was having trouble. The top of the list was relatively easy with former bosses and coworkers and a few people who didn't get the jobs they applied for, but after a handful of names, she was drawing a blank.

She groaned and pushed her chair back. She stretched her neck from side to side, loosening the tight muscles. Maybe she could book a massage before the launch. God knew she needed it. She laughed to herself. Like she had free time.

A massage was a luxury, sort of like a date was. She couldn't remember the last time she went on a date. As she got closer to her dream coming true, men were less and less important to her. And less and less willing to see her as a potential partner. Nope, she was a mark, someone to use for what they wanted. She was done being used.

Taylor considered going home, but she was too tired to drive. She kept a small closet of clothes in her office for the too many nights she stayed there. Her executive bathroom was almost as lavish as the one in her home, so she gave up the fight and moved from her desk chair to the couch that was even more comfortable than the one she had at home.

She sank back and closed her eyes. Deep breath in, and out. Again in, and out. She forced her mind to clear and let go of the day. Nothing was going to stop her from moving forward with her plans. Nothing.

Her phone rang, startling her out of her relaxed state. She wasn't asleep yet, but she was on her way. The price of running an online business.

Taylor answered without bothering to think about the blocked caller ID knowing many of her investors had blocked numbers. "Taylor Wright."

"Did you get my gift?" a man's voice asked.

"Who is this?" Taylor asked. Her voice trembled, and so did her hands. She looked around the silent office, feeling exposed.

"I wanted you to know I was thinking of you."

"What do you want?"

"I want you to appreciate me, Taylor. You wouldn't be where you are if it weren't for me. I want you to acknowledge that."

"Why don't you tell me who you are so I can?"

He chuckled. "That would be too easy. I understand, though. All the people you stepped on as you were climbing the ladder... It's easy to forget us all. But we never forgot about you."

"I didn't step on people."

His laugh sent ice to her heart. She shivered from the chill and grabbed her blanket.

"Taylor, Taylor, Taylor. You're so forgetful when it doesn't serve you. But I know exactly who you are. You're still that white trash who grew up on the wrong side of town. A cheap whore who tried to pretend she was someone she's not. But I know the real you, Tay-tay. I know everything about you. And I'm not going to let you destroy more lives."

"What are you talking about?" Taylor asked. Her mind raced to come up with a name. The list of people who knew her childhood nickname was short, but the voice... She couldn't place it.

He chuckled again, a breathy sound through the phone. "Don't play dumb with me. You're far too smart for it."

"I don't know what you're talking about."

"Yes, you do, Taylor. But I need to go now. We'll talk again very soon."

She tried to say something else, but he was gone. Taylor stared at her phone, shaking in her hand. The fear overtook her and the phone slid from her hand to the floor. She couldn't stop shaking.

The phone buzzed on the floor, making her jump. She looked at it as if it were a snake ready to strike. The screen lit up with an email. An update from a supplier.

Taylor drew a long breath, letting the air fill her lungs until they ached. She held it to the count of four, then slowly released the air. After a few more deep breaths, her hands stopped shaking and her heart slowed to normal. She picked up her phone and opened the email.

She didn't have time for threats. She had a job to do.

Read FUTURE today

ABOUT THE AUTHOR

USA TODAY Bestselling Author Mary E Thompson spent most of her childhood wishing she had a few less curves. She hid in the pages of books because her favorite characters never cared what size her clothes were. Now, neither does Mary, and she writes stories that celebrate women like her. Real women who have curves, chase dreams, and find love, because we should all be happy, no matter our dress size.

Mary spends her non-writing time with her husband and two kids, watching too much TV, cheering for her hometown football team (Go Bills!), and hiding chocolate from her family.

Visit https://MaryEThompson.com/subscribe/ to sign up for Mary's newsletter, **Romancing the Curves**. Subscribers get free ebooks and other fun stuff, like exclusive, members only content and giveaways, plus are the first to know about new releases and sales!

www.ingramcontent.com/pod-product-compliance
Lightning Source LLC
Chambersburg PA
CBHW031009190726
48286CB00003BA/763